SNIPER'S QUEST

The 7even series
MAINAK DHAR

A decorated special forces officer trying to forget the demons of his past and restart life in the civilian world. A legendary sniper, once on the frontlines of the war on terror and now hunted as a terrorist himself, on a mission to avenge his family.

Two men, two warriors, brought together by fate—destined to start as sworn enemies but end up as brothers in arms. In a world where the young and poor fight and die in wars started by the old and rich, they must join forces in a thrilling series of adventures to unravel the conspiracy that has put them, their loved ones and countless others in harm's way.

Sniper's Eye (2018)

I was out on a date. Everything was perfect… Till that shot… a high-calibre one, no apparent sound. And, the man in front of me fell. A rifle with a suppressor? A sniper in the middle of a Mumbai mall? As the body count mounted, I was soon sucked deeper into the chaos unleashed by that shot. To survive and save those whom I care about, I have to become the man I left behind. I have no choice but to tap into a bloody past that has put me on the terror kill list. I may also have no option but to join hands with the sniper terrorizing Mumbai. The problem is that the man has sworn to kill me.

'The action never leaves the pages even when there are no bullets flying or RPGs being fired. And it is for this reason that it is going to stay in my mind for a long time.'

—Arvind Passey,
Blogger and former Army Officer

'If this book were ever turned into a movie, then Akshay Kumar would be a perfect choice. Once you finish reading the book, you might just actually clap, stand up and say Vande Mataram.'

—Kitaabikeeda Blog

Praise for *Line of Control*

'Captures very well the cut and thrust of combat. A thrilling read.'

—General V.N. Sharma,
Former Chief of Army Staff

'By placing readers in the thick of action similar to the circumstances that we find ourselves in today, Dhar has actually managed to find a connect that cannot be missed easily.'

—HT City

'The spine-chilling war scenario entertains, by all means, with skilful plot, well-drawn variety of characters, thrilling action, a high degree of intrigue, suspense and tension, grim humour.'

—The Tribune

Praise for *Herogiri*

'Strikes a chord.'

—IBN Live

'The plot is engaging and wholesome Bollywood film material.'

'A delightful take on the superhero genre.'

'Excellent. Arnab "GA" Bannerjee is the unpretentious hero you want by your side...this affable, retiring 25-year-old is possibly the most likeable of all characters you shall meet this summer.'

'Here's a delightfully engaging take on the superhero genre. A racy roller coaster.'

'Exhilarating!'

SNIPER'S QUEST

A 7even Series Thriller

MAINAK DHAR

tara
India Research Press

tara
India Research Press

Flat. 6, Khan Market, New Delhi - 110 003
Ph: 24694610; Fax: 24618637
www.indiaresearchpress.com
contact@indiaresearchpress.com

2022

SNIPER'S QUEST

ISBN 13: 978-81-8386-194-6

Printed and Bound in India for
Tara Press·India Research Press

As always, for
Puja and Aaditya

Out of the night that covers me,
Black as the pit from pole to pole,
I thank whatever gods may be
For my unconquerable soul.

In the fell clutch of circumstance
I have not winced nor cried aloud.
Under the bludgeonings of chance
My head is bloody, but unbowed.

Beyond this place of wrath and tears
Looms but the Horror of the shade,
And yet the menace of the years.
Finds and shall find me unafraid.

It matters not how strait the gate,
How charged with punishments the scroll,
I am the master of my fate,
I am the captain of my soul.

—'Invictus' by William Ernest Henley

PROLOGUE

General Ghafoor poured himself a glass of Scotch. He leaned back on his sofa and looked out at the azure waters beyond his balcony. As the amber liquid made its way down his throat, he smiled and sighed. A long sigh of relief. Of victory. Of survival.

Little did he know that it would be the last drink he would ever have.

Ghafoor had been in the Pakistan Army for decades. Over time, he found himself involved in activities which had little to do with his job, but which proved immensely rewarding. He had first crossed paths with General Karimi when the man had showed up in Afghanistan for intel work with the Inter-Services Intelligence (ISI). Ghafoor had liaised with him. Ghafoor had soon been sucked into what he later knew as Operation Lotus. Karimi had told him how it would serve to expand Pakistan's sphere of influence, but Ghafoor later learned that it was ultimately about what drove most men—money, power, and ambition. That had served Karimi well, as he rose from being a general to becoming president of Pakistan. It had served Ghafoor well also, down to his penthouse in Dubai where he was this very moment.

He took another deep swig from the glass as he thought about the last few years. Things had been going well for everyone involved with Karimi and his plans. Money, women, scholarships for children, a life of luxury that would have been inconceivable to Ghafoor when he had begun his career more than two decades ago. All of those had over time helped him get over any initial pangs of conscience he might have had about being involved in what was, when you stripped it down, an operation to supply illicit drugs from Afghanistan to India and the West.

But all that had changed when a sniper blew apart Karimi's head with a single bullet.

Ghafoor remembered those days, and with those memories came a rising sense of panic as he emptied his glass and got up. He decided to pour himself another drink. Neat this time. He needed some fortification to still his shaking hands and slow his pounding heart.

Karimi's assassination had sparked panic. After all, it had not been the first time a Pakistani leader had met a violent death. The generals looked at each other suspiciously, marshalling their supporters, wondering who would make a grab for power. Many of Ghafoor's fellow generals had been in deep with Karimi on Project Lotus and owed their positions to the fact that they had helped Karimi, who in turn kept them close to him, knowing that he could not risk any of them betraying his secrets. They wondered who Karimi's successor would be.

General Parvez had died in Quetta when a single bullet

had taken him in the neck. Then General Akhtar had fallen near the Afghan border when the ISI team he was leading to hunt the sniper had been ambushed—and the hunters had turned into the hunted.

Ghafoor had never been in the ISI and was not privy to many of the secrets Karimi and his ISI men had, but realized pretty quickly that the sniper would soon be the least of his worries. The American attack on an Afghan compound a year ago had brought Project Lotus and the drug network run out of there into the public eye. Ghafoor read reports of people turning up dead, all shot by a sniper, and while he did not know all of them, he knew that quite a few of them had connections to Project Lotus.

If the sniper didn't get him, the Americans would. So Ghafoor had cashed in on old favours and moved to Dubai. Here, he was known as a businessman called Faisal. The last few months had been a welcome break and he had begun to think he had left his previous life behind.

That had been until General Rafique had died in Abu Dhabi three days ago, shot in the head while he sat on the beach.

Ghafoor set his glass down and looked at the screen on his mobile phone. It showed images from the CCTV cameras installed outside the apartment building and on his floor. His two Russian bodyguards stood just outside, armed with submachine guns, and he had another Russian in the adjoining apartment surveying footage from a drone he had flying overhead. Ghafoor had the money, he had the connections, and unlike some of his comrades, who had got fat and complacent from a life spent sitting behind a desk, he had been a career infantryman and had the tactical sense and experience to know that a whole platoon of Russian mercenaries outside his door would not stop a sniper of the calibre that may be on his trail. He just needed to get through the next twenty-four hours before he moved on to his next destination—Switzerland. He had his new identity, money in the bank there, and he would board the flight to Zurich the following day. His wife was with his sons in the United States and would join him later.

He called the Russian drone operator on his phone. 'Spotted anything? I told you to keep a watch on any boats or any suspicious movement on the beaches.'

The heavily accented voice came booming back. 'No, sir. Nothing to report. If you're okay, I'll bring the drone in for an hour to recharge it. There's nothing suspicious out there.'

Of course, that was where Ghafoor and the Russian got it terribly wrong.

Nine hundred metres away, a pigeon settled down on the blanket lying across the balcony of the hotel room on the twentieth floor. The official temperature during the day had been forty-three degrees, though old Dubai hands would tell you that the real temperature might well have been much higher. Now, at five in the evening, it had cooled quite a bit. The pigeon didn't need the weather report to tell it just how hot it had been over the last few days, and neither did the man lying under the blanket.

When they typically show a sniper lying in wait for his kill in the movies, they focus on the glamorous stuff that makes the hero look good—their quarry in their sights, the single shot, the exultation of the kill. For the man who lay in wait under the blanket, that was the easy part. All of that made up maybe ten seconds of activity. The harder part had been the eighty-six thousand, four hundred seconds he had been waiting, lying under the blanket, trying not to move, wearing adult diapers so he wouldn't need to get up to heed nature's call, drinking protein shakes and water through straws that snaked into containers tied to his back to keep his energy and hydration levels high, taking short naps so that he wouldn't be tired when the opportunity to take a clean shot came. Despite all that effort, he was beginning to cramp up, he was stinking, but he knew all of that was the price he would need to pay for success.

He had hidden in his lair when he'd heard from his informants that Ghafoor was planning to flee and was calling in Russian mercenaries to protect him. The Russians had been good. The idea of a drone circling above the building was a masterstroke, and it would have worked had a sniper been trying to get into position. The problem was that this sniper had not waited to get into position. He had checked into this hotel room as soon as he had got a tip-off about Ghafoor's plans and taken up his position before the first Russian had shown up or the security measures had kicked in.

Nothing was visible from the outside other than a few inches of the narrow barrel of his Dragunov sniper rifle, capped by the tubular suppressor. The blanket ended at the edge of his scope and through it he saw Ghafoor pour himself another drink.

People believe that snipers only think of the big picture, seeing a target from a long way off, dealing death impersonally from long range. This sniper knew better. He knew that success lay in the details. Such as the precise moment when the wind stilled, so that he would not have to factor in any major deviations in trajectory; when Ghafoor put his glass down to check his phone, so that the glass would not fall and shatter on the ground, alerting his guards outside; the fact that the sliding door to the balcony was open, something Ghafoor had done the previous day as well, perhaps to get an unhindered view of the sea.

Ghafoor looked out at the distant building gleaming in the evening sun. A luxury hotel, he supposed, arranged on the same sea-facing stretch of sand his apartment was on. Nothing lay in between for what seemed like a kilometre or more. So he had opened the balcony doors as he had done in previous evenings to enjoy the spectacular view with an incoming salty breeze minus the searing afternoon heat. He was about to lift up his glass when he spotted some movement.

A bird had taken off from one of the balconies in the hotel. No, that wasn't the only thing. He had caught the glint of sun on something. The Russian with his fancy drone might not have noticed it but Ghafoor's old combat instinct from years of being an infantry officer kicked in. He began to move, but it was all too little, too late.

The Dragunov has a muzzle velocity of 2,722 feet per second. In simple terms, that's the speed with which the 7.62mm calibre bullet leaves it. Gravity and air resistance do their bit to slow it down a bit as it reaches a long-range target, but the math makes the conclusion inescapable.

From the time the bullet left the rifle, it took just around a second to reach Ghafoor, entering just above his right eye and exiting out the back of his head. He slumped back on the sofa. Dead.

The shooter crawled back from under the blanket and back into the hotel room. The first thing he did was to strip and put his dirty clothing into a bag which he would carry with him and then dispose of at the airport. Then he took a long bath, washing the grime off himself. He looked at himself in the bathroom mirror. He had been a sniper for years, but he was not a monster, and every time he took a life he had to remind himself why he had done it. If he stopped asking that question, he knew he would indeed become a monster who revelled in the very act of taking lives. He was a devout Muslim, and his father would have told him that no man should judge anyone so harshly as to justify taking their life—judgement was Allah's prerogative.

However, his father, a gentle, kindly man, had been killed by the Taliban. Ghafoor, and others like him, had been part of an operation that had ruined hundreds of lives and fooled the Americans into launching drone strikes against targets they believed were terror targets, but were in reality just business rivals of Karimi. The sniper's mother had died in one of those strikes. No, some men did deserve to be judged, and he would seek forgiveness for his actions when he came before the Almighty in the afterlife, but in this life he would make those men pay for what they had done.

He carefully shaved the beard he had grown over the last month, and then dressed in a business suit. The rifle went into the guitar case in which it had been carried into the hotel. At the lobby downstairs, he checked out, smiling at the woman at the counter.

'How was the stay, Mister Azam?'

He rolled his eyes. 'As good as it could have been. The meeting I was hoping for never happened, but I enjoyed my time in my room, playing my guitar and watching the sea. As it happens, I'm meeting my client on the way to the airport.'

He left the hotel room and got into a waiting taxi. 'Airport, please.'

As the taxi sped off, Ghafoor's bodyguards came in to check on him, as he had not been answering their calls. They were less concerned about the fact that he was dead than they were about who would pay the balance of their fees. They didn't want to hang around when the body was found and the police called, so they discreetly packed up their things and left.

At the airport, the man who went by the name Azam did not enter the terminal. He had no intention of taking a flight from Dubai airport at any rate. He had no doubt his contacts had done a decent job with the forged passports, but this was not his field of expertise and he didn't know if the forgery was good enough to pass the scrutiny that might await inside. He walked out from the building to the agreed rendezvous point and got into a waiting car. They drove for over an hour into the desert. He briefly left the car to burn the bag with his dirty clothes and forged passport. The driver just waited silently as he completed his work, and then he got back inside.

An hour later, he was in the back of a truck, which would take him on a long journey to the Saudi border. From there he would be spirited out in yet another caravan. For the few seconds that had actually been involved in taking out both his targets in the United Arab Emirates, he had spent over two months in travelling, reconnoitering, hiding, and lying in wait. But then patience was an essential part of a sniper's toolkit, and he prided himself on being a very good one.

The others around him, a motley crew of smugglers and petty criminals, gave him a wide berth as he lay down and dozed. He was not a large man, and his Dragunov would have been of no use in such close quarters, but one of the men on the truck had fought in Afghanistan and recognized him. Whispers had swept through the back of the truck, and the men, many of them having fought in the wars in Afghanistan or in Iraq, or having had relatives who had fought there, or having smuggled weapons to one side or the other, knew who was travelling with them.

The sniper had his faults but being vain was not one of them. The day he let his head get too big, or started thinking he was the best, he would run into someone better than him, or just make a mistake and pay the price. However, today was not that day. As his eyes closed, he heard a man next to him whisper.

'Is that really the man they used to call Seven Six Two?'

Aman Karzai smiled and fell into a deep sleep.

You know you don't have a normal office job when your boss asks you to recover a colleague who has been kidnapped by pirates in the South China Sea.

Till that morning, I could have been forgiven for thinking that my days of rushing into harm's way were well behind me. Zoya and I had been married for close to two years, and our son, Aman, was close to a year and a half old. I had been working as a security consultant for Bharat Oil, one of the largest Indian oil companies. And after taking a break, Zoya had begun working full-time again. If you were to look at us from a distance, you might think we were just another young, middle-class couple living in Mumbai. You wouldn't guess the events that we had endured, events that had destroyed many lives and had almost left us both dead. Zoya and I tried not to talk about those days too much, yet there were times when we had to acknowledge that those days had had their lasting impact.

Like I said, I was understandably wary about the task my boss had for me.

Surjeet Singh Randhawa had once served in the Indian Navy, and behind the bulk he had put on after years of sitting in an office chair, you could still see the sharp eyes and ramrod-straight back that had served him well when he had been in uniform. I owed him a lot. He had offered me this job when I had perhaps been unemployable—a retired soldier whose face and name had been flashed all over television, first as a hero and then as someone who had allegedly committed war crimes. I knew he had done so at the behest of M.K. Dhar, a retired Intelligence Bureau spymaster who had reminded me that old men like him had many interesting connections. He had helped clear my name and, yes, he had helped me to get a new start with this job. Yet Randhawa could have easily rejected me, so I owed him.

Randhawa could see the hesitation in my eyes, and he leaned forward. 'Aaditya, I know you have a family and there's no way I would want you to get into harm's way. You'll be surprised at how routine this kind of stuff is in our line of business.'

That got my attention as he continued. 'It's an interesting part of the world. We're out there prospecting for natural gas, as are the Chinese, Filipinos, Vietnamese and God knows who else. You put a bunch of ships carrying civilians out there in waters that lots of countries claim, but nobody really polices, and you're asking for something like this to happen. Pirates occasionally board ships to rob them or to take hostages. We pay them off quietly and it's back to business.'

'Why don't we take the pirates out, sir? Our navy and others have done similar things near Somalia, and I remember piracy there came down a lot once they learned they could be the hunted, not the hunters.'

Randhawa smiled at me. 'You haven't lost your instinct for taking the fight to the enemy, have you? Here it is a bit more complicated. China claims these waters, as do a bunch of neighbouring countries. The US Navy sails through at times to wave the flag and show support for the Filipinos or Japs, and we are there both to look for resources and also to make a point to China that they can't take all of Asia as their backyard. A bit of flag-waving and posturing is good, but I doubt anyone wants to risk a shooting war with navies undertaking combat operations in there. Technically, China claims all those waters so they should be in charge. The fact that those pirates still operate, and they attack ships flying all sorts of flags other than the Chinese one, tells you something, doesn't it?'

Nothing ever really changed, did it? Since the first time I had put on a uniform and slipped into the night with my brothers to put ourselves in harm's way and to do harm to the enemies we were directed to kill, I had come to realize one simple truth—old men sitting in their comfortable offices played politics and games of power, but it was young fools like us who did the bleeding and dying.

I still hadn't said anything, and Randhawa must have thought I was going to refuse.

'Look, Aaditya, all I need you to do is some babysitting. Our finance director will head out with the money. Godbole is a very competent accountant, but not someone who's comfortable doing things like this. Making the accounts add up and dealing with pirates are two very different skillsets. Our previous security guy, who had served in the Gurkhas, went with him on the two previous occasions we've done this, and he had no more excitement on the trip than a big night out drinking with the Indian embassy folks in Hanoi. Also, you get a special bonus for this, and I know that can't hurt.'

'He's going to jump!'

Zoya turned towards me, half-asleep, and my vigilance was rewarded by a sharp elbow in my stomach. 'Aadi, go to sleep and please let me sleep.'

I managed to lie down, but I kept watching the video monitor a few inches from my face, seeing our son, Aman, moving around restlessly in his cot. He had started to move around with what I considered unwarranted confidence, and it was only a matter of time before he outgrew his crib. Twice in the previous week I had seen him at night, standing up, holding onto the crib's railings and trying to raise one foot over the edge, when I had rushed into his room, doing what Zoya laughingly called my night-time commando raids. Zoya would also joke that she hoped Aman inherited my height and outstripped my six feet three inches, but not my sense of adventure, of jumping into the unknown. We'd been planning to buy a new bed for Aman that weekend, but with my upcoming trip Zoya would now have to do it alone.

I turned towards Zoya, seeing the peaceful expression

on her face, her chest rising and falling gently as she slept, her hair falling across her face. I had gone into harm's way many times when I had donned my country's uniform, and at times our officers would exhort us to do so because families would be sleeping safer at home when we took out our targets. At the time, it had been an abstract concept for me. No longer.

At breakfast, I told Zoya about the upcoming trip, pirates and all. We had resolved that we would never keep secrets from each other and would share whatever came our way. Facing death together tends to bring you closer in a way love or passion alone cannot. She took it well enough, though the hint of a disapproving grimace formed at the corner of her mouth.

'Zo, I can see that pout coming. Just say it.'

She smiled, the grimace disappearing. 'I just don't want you in harm's way. Why can't they send someone else? Why do you need to head off on one more quest?'

I tried hard to not react with anger to her last sentence. I mean, it wasn't as if I had asked terrorists to start killing people in Mumbai or hijack the plane we were on. All I wanted to do was to live a simple life with my family. Didn't she get that?

She must have caught my expression and she gently touched my hand. 'I'm sorry, Aadi. I shouldn't have said that. It's just that I don't want you going into danger again. Don't they have anyone else to send?'

I had mentioned the same thing to Randhawa and told Zoya what the response had been.

'Godbole is a fat bureaucrat, and chances are the pirates will grab him if he goes in alone. Plus, I get a sense that Randhawa isn't sure how much to trust him with half a million dollars in cash.'

Zoya whistled when she heard the figure. 'And you're telling me this has happened before? How come we never read about it in the papers?'

'Politics.' I shrugged.

As Zoya got up to head for office, she looked back at me. 'That's what I'm worried about. Politics.'

'Dude, come here.'

Aman waddled over and held his arms open, wanting to be picked up. Everyone who saw him said he had inherited Zoya's looks and my height, which was perhaps a good thing, since I didn't know if I had any other positive genes to pass on. His hair was straight and wavy like Zoya's, unlike the unruly mop that was my bane. His skin was glowing like hers, though to be fair, I had forgotten what my skin had been like before years of atrocious conditions—crawling in the sand, freezing in the night, getting bitten by leeches in the forests—had reduced it to its now permanently tanned and parched state. As I held his soft, chubby hands with my calloused and gnarled ones, I felt a sense of responsibility that I had never felt before. Never had someone been so totally dependent on me.

As I strapped Aman in the child seat and began to drive to his preschool to drop him before I went to work, he smiled at me. Zoya had felt a bit guilty about going back to work so soon, but she had got a great offer and I had told her candidly that she was far better qualified and educated than me to get a great job and help provide for the kind of future and education we'd want Aman to have. I found that being the one who stayed at home more than she did and taking more care of Aman with my flexible working hours had made me appreciate that being a homemaker and taking care of a baby was no easier than going to an office.

Whenever I looked at Aman, I couldn't help but be reminded of the man in whose honour I had named my son. An enigma of a man, a ruthless sniper to some, a wanted killer to others, but to me a comrade in arms, an honourable man who had tried to come to grips with his bloody past by waging a lonely battle against those who had destroyed his life. Many like Karimi were dead now. But there were countless others—the shadowy Chinese Unit 7 we had encountered in Afghanistan, for example.

While I tried to get my life back to normalcy, he had been keeping busy. Every once in a while, I'd see a news report of a mysterious sniper shooting—of an Afghan general, of a Pakistani businessman, a Chinese triad boss. At first, I had not given them much thought, but over the months they'd added up. I had a collection of those headlines tucked away in a folder on my laptop. Every single one of those killings bore the hallmark of Aman Karzai. A man whose credo was 'one shot, one kill'. I didn't know how long he would keep going, but he had committed himself to a life of hunting those who had once hunted us.

Aman looked at me and beamed, the locket given by Karzai around his neck. When Aman was older, maybe he would ask where the locket had come from, and I would tell him of the man who had put it around his neck on a dusty hill in Afghanistan.

'Dada, we play bang bang.'

'Sure, we will.'

Of all the things Zoya wished Aman hadn't inherited from me, the worst was his love for smashing his toys together—whether they be cars or stuffed animals, he made them collide in imaginary battles, pretending they were blowing each other to smithereens. I guessed I hadn't helped when I had taught him how to use his penguins to flank his monkeys or how to set up the best possible ambush for his tractors.

Yes, no matter what his looks were, he was his father's son all right.

I had never really met Godbole before, other than being briefly introduced to him when I had joined. He was an Indian Revenue Service officer and had spent many years in the Finance Ministry and was thus much better connected to the government machinery than Randhawa was. That, perhaps even more than his role as finance director, meant that he was entrusted with these missions. I had learned from long experience that I didn't have to like someone to be able to work with them. I could only hope that Godbole subscribed to a similar philosophy because we got off on entirely the wrong foot from the moment we were formally introduced by Randhawa, and he was told that I would be accompanying him.

'A soldier? Really, Randhawa, we should get someone more used to diplomatic negotiations and niceties.'

'Godbole, there will be someone from the Indian embassy accompanying you. Plus, when dealing with pirates, you may need someone who has more deterrent value than the fancy sentences he can string together.'

Randhawa said it pleasantly enough, but I couldn't hide the smile that crept onto my face as he put Godbole in his place. I thought I had wiped the smile off my face but he glared at me.

'Last time it was that Gurkha who took his khukri with him and kept displaying it. Most unprofessional.'

This time I couldn't help but laugh loudly. 'Sorry, sir. But that Gurkha sounds like my kind of man.'

He glared at me even more and I decided to offer him an olive branch. 'I'm just there as your escort, sir. You take all the decisions and do all the talking. I'm just there to make sure you're safe.'

Godbole straightened, happy to get what he considered appropriate respect from someone beneath his station. He stood a good six inches shorter than me, and his double chin and bulging belly didn't help him command much by way of respect or authority, but he nodded at me sagely. I had to force myself not to laugh at this peacock showing his frayed feathers.

'That's better. We'll do just fine, I think.'

As he strode off, Randhawa patted me on my shoulder. 'Nicely done. I would have told him to bugger off.

Bureaucrats come by here, thinking this is another ministry junket, only to learn that we are trying to run a company as professionally and profitably as we can.'

'No worries, sir. A wise CO once told me to not piss off bureaucrats unless we really had to. He said many of them are like mushrooms—they grow well in shit, and some of them can be extremely poisonous.'

Zoya folded my clothes and put them in my bag. She hadn't spoken much that evening. I knew that was a bad sign. She was normally the talkative one and it was always uncomfortable when I found myself doing most of the talking.

I was carrying Aman, following her around as she put things in my bag. 'Zo, it's a two-day trip. I won't need half the clothes you've put in there.'

She looked back at me. Her eyes were brimming over with tears. Aman could sense the change in mood, and he began bawling. I had not been married or had a kid when I had served, and now I wondered how those who did ever managed to say their goodbyes when they were headed out on missions of the sort we undertook. Here I was, going on a business trip, and it felt like I was headed out across the Line of Control. I took her hand and sat down next to me. Aman was now looking at us, trying to understand what his parents were up to, since he normally did all the crying in the house.

'Aadi, I don't ever want you to be in the kind of danger you have been in the past. Promise me you won't rush into anything this time.'

I remembered our first date, which had been interrupted when the man in front of us had been shot and I had rushed off to find the shooter. Could I honestly promise that faced with the same situation, I would run and hide? Would I be fair to those who counted on me?

'All I want to do is continue our life the way it is, with you and Aman. That's all. I won't do anything that threatens that. I promise you that, Zo.'

She smiled and held me close, and Aman cooed. As I held my family in my arms, I wondered just how much I'd be able to live up to my promise. I had stopped seeking out trouble. The problem was that trouble seemed to have an annoying knack of seeking me out.

Our flight landed in Hanoi at ten in the night, almost an hour after its scheduled time of arrival. Adding a four-hour layover in Bangkok, I had spent close to fourteen hours in a plane or in airports and was looking forward to getting some sleep. Godbole seemed to be in better shape, but then after putting away three glasses of Scotch, he seemed to have slept through most of the trip.

We were greeted outside the arrivals gate by a man whom I immediately knew was more than what he claimed to be. He was about my age, though with more of his hair missing, pretty fit for a supposedly middle-aged bureaucrat, with a lean, toned physique, a ramrod-straight posture and when he shook my hand, I could feel a strong grip.

'Good evening, Major Aaditya Ghosh. My name's Sandeep Krishnan, and I'm the cultural attaché here.'

My thoughts of getting sleep were soon thrown out the window because Krishnan insisted that we get a proper briefing before our trip the next afternoon. As it turned out, the briefing ended up being an excuse for him and Godbole to drink and catch up over old times.

We were sitting at the rooftop bar of the Renaissance Riverside Hotel we were booked at, and when Krishnan ordered Johnnie Walker Gold Label, I couldn't help but wonder what kind of expense account he was on.

'Ghosh, a drink for you?'

'Just black coffee.'

He looked at me incredulously and Godbole sniggered. 'Good soldier and all. Guess he doesn't drink on duty.'

Krishnan raised his glass to me and took a sip of his drink. As he and Godbole chatted about past trips together, I realized that they had done this before.

Something struck me when Krishnan laughed out loud when Godbole mentioned his last trip here to deliver ransom money to pirates and I caught them exchanging a knowing glance. Randhawa must have started sending his man with them not just for Godbole's security but to ensure that these two gentlemen weren't taking some of the ransom money for themselves on the side. To be honest, there was little I could do on that count, since the money was to be delivered by the local embassy and Krishnan could skim a little before handing the money over to Godbole to give to the pirates, but at least there was some sort of checks and balances with someone there other than just these two pals sitting together.

'Something amusing you, Ghosh?'

I had promised Zoya that I wouldn't rush into trouble, but I didn't need to take lip from a corrupt bureaucrat. 'No, Krishnan. How long have you been in RAW? You don't look the way you do by sitting behind a desk all your life. So, I guess an army or police officer who somewhere along the way thought being a spy was way cooler and more rewarding.'

He just smiled, raising his glass to me again. 'Very good. You're obviously observant, and yes, sometimes the poor cultural or agricultural attachés are the ones who have the least to do with cultural exchanges or sharing agricultural best practices. Leave me, though. You've had a far more interesting life and career, Major. Cross-border raids, featuring on jihadi kill lists. I just hope you don't bring your penchant for attracting trouble to my humble little post. It's been a nice stint here—good people, good weather, and good food...'

He had clearly done his homework on me and I raised my cup to him. To his homework and to his vocabulary. What self-respecting soldier says 'penchant' to another grunt? Definitely not a soldier. A police officer who became a spook, then.

Godbole was watching us, feeling suddenly cut out of the conversation, and ordered one more glass before clapping his hands together to get our attention. 'Now, gentlemen. Shall we talk of some pirates?'

I might have had reservations about Krishnan's honesty, but there was little doubt about his competence. The next morning, we seemed to have a veritable parade of Vietnamese officers and troops at our hotel, and we left in a convoy of black Mercedes SUVs.

Krishnan, Godbole and I were in one car, driven by a silent, dour-faced Vietnamese driver who didn't say a single word. There were two more SUVs flanking us, each carrying three soldiers armed with assault rifles. One of them also had an officer, who other than shaking my hand said nothing all morning. Seeing the amount of firepower that was accompanying Godbole and Krishnan to the exchange, I was convinced that Randhawa didn't need me to keep Godbole safe and it reinforced my suspicion that he had started sending someone he could trust, usually an ex-serviceman employed as a consultant, to ensure that Godbole was kept as honest as possible.

Godbole was very talkative that morning, yammering on about all sorts of topics, while Krishnan was silent. I was sitting next to the driver and managed to catch his eye in the rear-view mirror once and he just nodded at me. That told me a lot about him. Amateurs react to stress through hyperactivity and chatter; professionals just prepare silently.

Our convoy stopped at a military airfield and we were

whisked off towards three waiting helicopters. As we took off, I caught Krishnan's eye again.

'Doesn't all this hardware spook the pirates?'

'On the contrary, Major. They respect a bit of a show of force. If we just went in as bureaucrats carrying a ransom, they'd probably kidnap us as well. You'll see what I mean.'

An hour later, after having flown over an endless procession of islands dotted with trees and bereft of any signs of civilization, I could see grey-coloured ships in the distance. By their sleek silhouettes, I guessed they were naval vessels. Our chopper banked towards an island, which lay was between two groups of ships. As we landed and I jumped out, I could see several Vietnamese soldiers waiting for us. The Vietnamese officer who had accompanied us, a Major Drang from the introduction Krishnan had given, came and stood just a few feet away. I pointed to the grey ships ahead of us.

'Your ships, Major?'

He smiled, revealing yellowing teeth. 'Chinese.'

Wasn't this one cosy neighbourhood? You had Indian spies, Vietnamese troops and helicopters, pirates and now Chinese warships.

'What are they doing here?'

Drang smiled again, even more broadly this time. 'Just our usual games. They pick up our choppers on radar and send ships to show us these islands are theirs. Of course, we have a base here and as the Americans say, possession is nineteenth-tenths of the law, right?'

I got the point and didn't have the heart to correct his mangled aphorism. Nor did I have the time as two black Zodiac craft roared into view, stopping at the beach just a few metres from us. Four men got out of the first Zodiac, carrying assault rifles and with RPG launchers slung across their backs. They were wearing jeans and t-shirts and other than their deadly arsenal could have been mistaken for being just another bunch of good-for-nothing street toughs. As they came closer, I caught the whiff of marijuana. The biggest of them, perhaps as tall as me, stood near us and began jabbering in Vietnamese. Scars crisscrossed his bare arms, the stench of alcohol was so strong it carried to us, and several pearl necklaces were strung across his muscular and broad neck and chest. His face was covered in a scarf, which revealed nothing but his eyes.

They had asked me to stand back, behind the chopper. Drang was talking in a conciliatory tone with the pirates. Once in a while, Krishnan would butt in with the occasional phrase, rarely getting beyond his first sentence before he was interrupted. I couldn't help but smile at this thug's show of bravado, and at how I had absent-mindedly wondered on the way what a modern-day pirate looked like. Give me Johnny Depp's version any day over this drugged-out, drunk lout.

The pirate leader shook his head at something Drang said and then he saw me. He kept staring at me, even when Krishnan or Drang were addressing him.

What was with this guy?

Krishnan, realizing that the pirate seemed fixated on me, signalled subtly for me to come closer. I had no idea what he had told the pirate I was, but apparently, the man wanted me to show myself more clearly. The moment I came closer, I could sense a change in his mood. His eyes widened, as if in recognition. Then he quickly recovered and got on with the negotiations. Krishnan pointed at me, and then translated for my benefit.

'I'm telling them you're a government officer who's flown in from Delhi and we need to hurry as you're on a schedule.'

The large pirate stared at me. Krishnan was whispering something to me, but the man shut him up with a raised finger and then addressed me and then pointed towards Godbole.

'You soldier? Don't look like desk-humper like this fat man.'

Godbole reddened and I laughed back. 'Doesn't matter who I am. Now unless you want to call the Chinese over and have a proper party, get us our men, take your money and let's all get back to whatever we would rather be doing.'

I was watching the man's eyes all this time and something didn't add up for me. He was dressed the part all right, but unlike the other men with him, his eyes were razor-sharp, showing an intelligence that I didn't see in the others with him. I thought I saw something familiar in those eyes but couldn't really think of how I could have crossed paths with a South China Sea pirate. He was big but with evenly developed muscles that indicated constant exercise and effort, not trips to the gym to just build up biceps. Come to think of it, the way he stood, the way he carried himself—just as he had called me out, I could spot a fellow soldier.

He caught the look in my eye and motioned for one of his men to go to the second Zodiac. The man removed a tarpaulin cover on the boat and brought out three people—two men and a woman with their hands tied behind them. As they came over to us, Vietnamese soldiers rushed to them while Krishnan handed over a suitcase.

'The money's all there. No need to count.'

The pirate laughed. 'No, no need to count. If you cheat, next time we kill instead of exchanging. Right?'

As we walked back to the helicopters, the three Indian hostages were being checked by a medic at the helipad. They seemed to be in good enough shape and they thanked us as we passed them. The woman caught my eye. She was perhaps forty, a few years older than me, and carried herself with a quiet dignity that told me she was used to being in charge. However, when she spoke, her voice cracked, betraying the stress she was under.

'Anita Padmanabhan. I was the captain of the survey ship that was taken. I was in the navy before I took premature retirement, and I can recognize a fauji when I see one. I saw and heard how you handled that bastard pirate. You're in the army, right?'

I was about to tell her that my days in the army were well behind me when she leaned towards me. 'Thank God they sent a soldier. You may appreciate what I have…I will try to get in touch with you.'

She stumbled, and I reached out to steady her. She gripped my hands with a terrible strength, and I could see tears well up in her eyes. Before she could say any more, Krishnan ushered her away and towards one of the helicopters.

As the first helicopter took off, carrying the freed hostages and Godbole, Krishnan winked at me. 'Mission accomplished. As easy as that.'

Before boarding our helicopter, I turned and saw the pirate leader still staring at me. He then undid the scarf, and I felt my heart in my mouth as I recognized the man.

The last time I had seen him had been in an abandoned US post in Afghanistan, where I had been tied up and tortured by his underlings. Clearly, he had survived the bloodbath there, but what was he doing here? He was no pirate. He was, from whatever I had gathered, an officer in a secret Chinese special forces group called Unit 7.

As our helicopter turned away, the man had a grin on his face and extended his right arm, his index finger and thumb making the shape of an imaginary gun. The thumb came down like an imaginary hammer as he fired. The gun might have been make-believe, but the malice in his eyes was real.

As the helicopter flew away, I felt something I had not felt in a very long time. The adrenaline rush of combat mixed with fear.

'Did you find out whether they kept their ransom money in an old-fashioned pirates' chest?' Ravi Mathur had had one wine too many, and the volume of his laughter was increasing in inverse proportion to the decreasing quality of his jokes.

The day after I had returned, Zoya had called Ravi and his wife Rekha over for dinner. Ravi had once trained me and was the closest thing to a father I had when I had lost both my parents soon after I had joined the Indian Army's Para Special forces. He had kept me going then, and later in life when I realized I could not take safety and anonymity for granted. Ravi had become my trainer once again, helping me get my mind and body back into the shape they had been when I had been a Para.

After dinner, Ravi had taken me aside, handing me a glass of wine. 'Looks like you've learned to prefer the company of pirates to us.'

I had known Ravi long enough to know that he

wanted to know what was on my mind. It would have been difficult to explain what I felt to anyone else, but Ravi would understand. I told him about the pirate leader, and I could see he was disturbed.

'Chances are he is a mercenary. When you told me all that had happened in Afghanistan, I doubted whether the Chinese would send their own elite troops there. He's probably someone who went over to the private sector for the bigger bucks. It could just be a coincidence. I doubt you'll ever see him ever again. But tell me how did you feel when you recognized him? You actually enjoyed it, right? Brought back a feeling of being in the zone again. I guess at some level, people like us miss being at war, no matter what we say.'

I looked up sharply at Ravi. He chuckled and poured himself another glass of wine.

'I've been out of the forces much longer than you, and I can tell you, when you do the crazy stuff we did for so many years, it's hard to ever truly reconcile to what civilians call a normal life. For years, I'd duck for cover when I heard a loud sound. I'd wake up in the middle of the night, shouting for the squad to take cover. Once, a small-time thief tried to grab Rekha's handbag. I broke his hand. Rekha actually took me to see a shrink when the cops told me they wouldn't press charges if I got help in view of my service in the Army. Post-traumatic stress disorder, apparently.'

I'd had no idea Ravi had been through all this. I had always seen him as invulnerable, the officer who led his men into hell and back, who never lost his aura even as his hair whitened and his body became slightly bent with age. I thought back to all the nights I had woken up in a sweat, dreams of dead men filling my head. Of those times I had found myself blanking out, remembering a comrade who had died in my arms. Of the times when my fingers would stray to an old scar and trigger an avalanche of memories. Memories drenched in blood. I hadn't gone for therapy or done yoga, and I'd never really drunk all that much, but I realized I had found my own way of recovering from my past.

My family.

As if reading my thoughts, Zoya sat next to me, wrapping her arms around me. 'No more herogiri, Major saab. Okay?'

I kissed her forehead. 'All I did was babysit a fat babu. No herogiri required, and I'm perfectly happy without it in my life.'

Out of the corner of my eye, I could see Ravi smirk, but I ignored him as Aman waddled up and I picked him and put him on my lap. Rekha walked in, carrying a plate piled with freshly made pakodas. As I picked one up, Ravi turned on the TV. Varsha Singh was on, her channel ICTV having been the one that had splashed my photos all over television, leading to the dubious distinction of featuring me on a jihadi kill list. I had hated her then, but over time had come to realize that she had just been doing her job.

'Reports are coming in of Indian and Chinese troops once again locked in an eyeball-to-eyeball confrontation on the border. Chinese troops crossed the Line of Actual Control and tried to dismantle an Indian post. Indian troops intervened. Words were exchanged, and the ugly situation was defused only with the intervention of senior officers. Such a peaceful resolution has not always been the case when it comes to these two nuclear-armed Asian giants.'

Varsha looked at the camera and paused. I could sense she had another of her scoops coming.

'We have got exclusive video footage, apparently from a couple of years ago of another confrontation in the same area, when things did escalate to a physical altercation. Both Indian and Chinese officials have refused to comment on the authenticity of the video, but the facts cannot be denied.'

A grainy video began airing on the screen. I could see several Chinese soldiers pointing and shouting. A Sikh soldier walked towards them, palms held outwards in a conciliatory gesture. Suddenly, a tall figure moved ahead of the Chinese soldiers towards the Indian and there was a flash of movement. The Indian soldier stumbled back, holding his face. Four more Indian soldiers charged ahead, arms and legs flying. The Chinese joined in the melee. Just before the video ended, I caught a glimpse of the tall man who had struck the Indian soldier. He was looking straight at the camera.

It was a grainy visual, but unmistakable. The same man I had run into just a few days earlier.

———×———

A week passed. The trip to Vietnam had all but faded from memory. I thought of the man from time to time, but perhaps Ravi was right. He had clearly been in the Chinese army but to show up in Afghanistan and then among pirates in the South China Sea, perhaps he had become a gun for hire. A dangerous man, but with no way of getting to me and my family. I saw no reason to alarm Zoya and tried to put him out of my mind.

Between days at work, evenings with Zoya and Aman, and the self-defence classes I held in the neighbourhood, I had hardly any time to think of more. My life returned to the normalcy I so craved. That was till Randhawa called me into his office.

'Aaditya, I'm worried about something that involves one of our employees. As head of security, I thought I'd get your advice before I did anything like call the police.'

Randhawa was not one to be easily worried, so the fact that he was contemplating calling the cops got my attention. As I sat, he placed a personnel folder in front of me.

There were employment details and a photograph. It was a photograph of the woman I had met in Vietnam. The same distraught-looking woman who had spoken to me briefly when she had been released by the pirates.

Anita Padmanabhan.

'Aaditya, Anita was one of our best and while I can understand her being shaken after her ordeal, it's not like her to act like this. She wrote me a mail soon after she got back saying she'd like some time off but would return this week. She never showed up and isn't responding to calls or emails. Finally, when I managed to speak to her, she sounded really stressed. I wanted to ask whether we should go to the police, or am I overreacting?'

'Boss, she was kept hostage by pirates. I can't imagine it's left her with very good memories. Maybe she just needs some time off.'

Randhawa was toying with a paperweight on his desk, spinning it. I knew he was weighing something in his mind. So I waited.

'Aaditya, I was hesitating because I don't want to involve you in anything that could become tricky or get you mixed up in anything that makes you uncomfortable. I know what you've been through...'

'I am head of security here. It's my job to get involved if one of our employees is in an unsafe situation. Tell me everything. You're leaving something out.'

'She hasn't returned any of my calls after our last chat, but sent me a text message asking who the soldier was who came to rescue her. When I told her, she wrote back saying she remembered you from the news.'

I sensed what was coming even before Randhawa said the words. 'She says she will speak only to you.'

———————

Anita Padmanabhan's voice came across the phone in barely a whisper. I wondered if she was seriously unwell or something else was going on.

'Ms Padmanabhan? Aaditya Ghosh. We met at that island...'

There was a pause before she responded. 'Thank God

it's you. I didn't know who else to reach out to. I thought a
soldier could ensure what I have gets into the right hands.
When Randhawa told me your name, I was sure you were
the right person to help me.'

I realized she was slurring a bit. She sounded dead
tired, as if she hadn't got much sleep.

'When I was locked up, the two men with me were
scared and kept to themselves, going on and on about how
they'd quit when they got back home. I was scared as well
but I noticed things that they did not. Maybe it was my
training, or maybe it was just me trying to focus on doing
something so I didn't lose my mind.'

She paused, as if trying to work up the courage to keep
going. 'The pirates fed us regularly, and never roughed
us up. We knew they'd release us when they got their
ransom, but they weren't so easy on the other captives.
They may have called themselves pirates but they were too
well organized. They were running a tight ship. There were
regular guard rotations. Some of the men were riffraff, but
most of them seemed disciplined and knew what they were
doing. That pirate leader you met during the exchange,
for instance. Some of them must have been soldiers at one
time or the other.'

I had already guessed as much. 'You mentioned them
not being easy on some of the captives. What makes you
think that?' I asked, trying to get her to come to the point.

'I saw stains on the walls of our cell. Dried blood. Some
of the previous occupants had scratched messages on the
wall. And of course, we heard screams at night once in a
while. I knew they would let us go, but I wasn't going to

just sit there at their mercy, so I began to see if there was any way we could escape. I didn't have a serious plan, but it gave me something to do. The guys with me kept trying to discourage me, saying it would anger our captors, but I didn't have much else to do, did I? I spotted a part of the wall that seemed to be chipped away, and when I dug into it with my fingernails, it came clean off, revealing a small hole to the adjoining cell.'

I was hearing her speak with growing admiration. She had been through hell, yet she had borne her captivity with discipline and courage that would have done any of my former comrades proud.

Then she came to what was bothering her. 'There was a man there, who asked who I was. When I told him, he was delirious with joy at finding a fellow Indian, that too a hostage who was likely to be released soon.'

'He was Indian?'

Her voice again came down to a whisper, and the growing confidence I had heard in the last few seconds seemed to disappear. 'Yes, Indian. His voice was nothing more than a croaked whisper. I could barely understand what he said, but he passed me a piece of paper, telling me to give it to someone senior in the Indian government or army. I kept asking him who he was, and he would laugh and say he would not reveal who he was, other than what he had put on the piece of paper. I told someone at the embassy in Vietnam. He sounded concerned enough and polite enough, but he clearly did nothing. Absolutely nothing. So I assumed I'd need to write to the government here to get things moving. I wrote to the Ministry of

External Affairs as soon as I came back, and you know what they did? I sent them a scan of the paper along with a long statement of my experiences. They didn't even send me an acknowledgement! Nobody seemed to pay any attention. Then a few days ago, someone began to follow me. I could sense it when I went out. Once or twice, I thought I saw the same guy behind me. The bastard wasn't even making an attempt to hide. I came back home one night and was sure someone had been there, going through my things. My things were messed around with a bit, not something you would notice on the face of it, but a message to me, like the batteries being taken out of my TV remotes. They've also been threatening me to keep quiet.'

I gripped my phone hard. Anita Padmanabhan needed help. She may have encountered another captive where she had been kept hostage, but it was stretching credibility to believe that someone was tormenting her the way she was describing. With the trauma she had been through, she most likely may have been suffering from post-traumatic stress disorders (PTSD) episodes that made her believe that someone was still out to get her.

'Anita, have you considered seeing someone? You've been through hell of a sort. I know a number of my buddies who got counselling to help them cope with what they'd been through while they served.'

She spat out her reply. 'You condescending bastard! I don't need a doctor. I need someone to care enough to do something about this paper I found, and the man who I met there.'

I heard a glass shatter. 'Anita, are you okay?'

She was in tears when she replied, 'No, I'm not okay. Someone has been threatening me. I've had my house burgled, I've been followed around and I've got anonymous notes showing up in my SMS and email inboxes saying I should burn the paper and forget it. My father served in the army and died serving this nation. I served in uniform as well, and I cannot forget this. All I want is for someone to act on my information, but in trying to do that I've put myself in a lot of danger. I thought as an officer, you could help me.'

'If all this is happening, go to the cops.'

She laughed, a bitter sound. 'I called the cops and told them I was coming. When I opened the door of my house, I found a dead black cat there. Its head had been cut off. I have no idea how they're doing this. Maybe they're tapping my phone, maybe they're watching me. Now I'm hiding somewhere they can't find me. I can't go back to my house. I just need to get this paper to someone who can do something with it. Please help me.'

I took a deep breath. I wasn't sure I could provide the sort of help Anita needed. It sounded so fantastic—finding secret notes, being followed, her phone being tapped and now a dead cat on her doorstep. I barely knew her and the last thing I wanted to do was to throw my life into chaos by getting involved in something that wasn't my business.

'Ms Padmanabhan, I know a senior officer in the police whom I could call. If you're not feeling safe, he could help.'

I heard a long sigh. A sigh of resignation. A sigh of disappointment. 'Yeah, I hear you. Nobody wants to get involved, right? Get on with your life, but if you have served in the forces, you may regret not seeing what I had. Too bad.'

'Look, it's not that I don't believe you. But if you need to get something to the government, you must know how slowly the bureaucracy works. Maybe they will get around to it. Just hang in—'

Anita Padmanabhan had hung up.

A couple of days went by in the kind of blur it can only do when you have a young child at home. Aman's antics meant that I almost had no time to think about what had happened.

It was a Friday. My evenings were spent at the community centre of a nearby apartment complex where I taught self-defence. Being a consultant to Bharat Gas had its perks—one of them was getting home at a very decent hour to both spend time with family and try to help others around me. I did a class in the afternoons after picking up Aman from preschool and another in the evenings. Zoya sometimes joined the evening classes after she got back. While we never spoke about it, I knew her motivation came from having been abducted and not wanting to feel so helpless ever again. If I was honest, my doing these classes was not just born out of an altruistic desire to help others, but to ensure that I kept myself sharp.

That Friday, she had taken Aman over to a neighbour's

house for a play date and I was with eight of my students, ranging from three young kids to a grandmother.

One of the students, a rather precocious twelve-year-old called Ryan, raised his hand. 'Sir, my sensei said we should never hit the face.'

I knew he learned karate at a nearby club. I didn't want to disrespect what his teacher was teaching him. 'He's absolutely right, Ryan. In the karate dojo you're not trying to hurt each other. When you spar with your friends you should not hit the face. However, here we're trying to learn what we can do if we are forced to defend ourselves on the street and there being polite and concerned about your attacker's safety or looks won't get you far.'

Everyone laughed at my joke, but Ryan's eyes lit up. I knew he was a bit of a scrapper and the prospect of being taught how to fight was appealing to him. So I could see his enthusiasm dampen at what I told him next.

'Punching someone in the face may mean you end up with a broken or fractured hand. Or, if you do some serious injury to your attacker, you may end up in the police station. My recommendation—if in doubt, scream for help, kick the attacker between the legs and run as fast as you can. The best self-defence in the real world is to keep yourself safe with minimal harm to all concerned.'

Everyone laughed again.

After we wrapped up, I got home, showered and changed and was about to leave to pick up Zoya and Aman, when my mobile phone rang.

It was Anita Padmanabhan. 'Have you changed your

mind? Are you willing to help me?'

I closed my eyes. I had told Randhawa about my call with her, leaving out some of the more fantastic portions, but recommending that she get some urgent medical help. He had thanked me and told me that there was nothing more I could do for her.

'Anita, I am very willing to help, but all this about a note, people following you around…'

There was a brief silence before she continued. 'I guess I have to do this myself. You know what's most disappointing? Not once did you ask me what was on the paper. You just assumed I was crazy or paranoid. I come from an army family, that's why I know the possible value of what was on the paper. If nobody is willing to do anything, I am on my way to Varsha Singh's studio. I told her I might have a scoop for her. She was pretty keen to learn what I had when I hinted at it having potentially huge ramifications. Being someone who has just been kidnapped by pirates does, it seems gives her a good "hook", whatever that means. Maybe media attention may get the government to do something. Wish me luck.'

I could hear the disappointment in her voice as she hung up. As I drove to pick up Zoya, I felt a headache coming on, and later, as we were sitting at the restaurant, Zoya asked me if I was feeling well. I told her I was fine, but I wasn't. I looked at Zoya and Aman and convinced myself that I had done the right thing, that I needed to live for them, that I owed them a normal life, not one where they had to worry about me coming home alive each day. That part of my life was behind me, and after all I had seen,

I was not going to rush into danger. I certainly wasn't going to go off on a quest because some woman I hardly knew claimed to have some secret note and was being stalked by imaginary enemies.

Zoya looked at me, seeing through any attempt at concealment I could have put up. 'What's bothering you?'

I hesitated, not really sure where to begin.

She put her hand over mine. 'Aadi, we promised each other. No more secrets.'

I looked at Aman. He was too young to understand what I was going to say, but I'd feel more comfortable if he was busy doing and seeing something else. Zoya understood my glance and whipped out her phone and put on some cartoon Aman was soon immersed in, blissfully oblivious to everyone and everything else happening around him.

I told Zoya everything that had happened. 'Zo, on the one hand, I did everything I should have done. I checked up on her and reported back to my boss. That's really what my job description would have me do. But why is something still bothering me?'

Zoya held my hand tightly. 'Maybe it's because you aren't the kind of man who limits himself to his job description. She could be in trouble. She's probably making things up or hallucinating about these people following her around and this note she supposedly found, but alone, in this mental state, she could hurt herself.'

'Do you want me to get involved? After all we've been through...'

Aman looked up from the screen in front of him and

smiled. I smiled back at him and as he beamed, I reached out to ruffle his hair.

'Aadi, I don't want to tell you to do anything. Certainly, I don't want you to go into harm's way, but please don't stop from following your instinct because you're thinking about us. Whatever you do, I'll be there for you, and if this Anita needs help, maybe it won't be such a bad idea to meet her once. Maybe it'll calm her down a bit.'

I thought it over and took out my phone to call Anita. I dialled her number, but got a message saying that her number was not reachable. I tried a couple of more times with the same result and then gave up.

We went home and soon worries about Anita and the note receded from my mind as I got busy playing with Aman. Today, he had discovered the ability to blow bubbles with his spit and was doing them, giggling delightedly as he blew a bubble and it burst.

'Aadi, that is disgusting!'

I could see Zoya's point but seeing Aman's eyes open in wonder and the smile on his face prevented me from stopping him. One day he would grow up. One day he would realize that the world wasn't filled with people who loved him. But till then, he was all mine. I couldn't change the world, but in my small way, I could help him see more of the good than the bad. Perhaps that was all we could really do as parents, wasn't it?

I stroked his head, and he smiled back. 'Dude, want to blow up some dinosaurs?'

He nodded enthusiastically and we got down to

business. An F-16 was about to dive down for an attack on a T-Rex when Zoya called out to me from the living room.

'Aadi. Come here. Quick.'

I knew from her tone something was wrong. I ran to the living room. She was in front of the TV, and the news was on. The visuals showed several cars piled up on the Western Express Highway and the anchor's voice cut through.

'As we have been reporting, there has been a major accident in Mumbai just one hour ago. One person has been confirmed killed and four others injured on the Western Expressway.'

A face flashed on the screen. I was shocked.

The anchor continued. 'The deceased is reported to be Anita Padmanabhan, a former naval officer, who worked at a major oil and gas company. Police sources report that they have found high levels of alcohol in her body and that may have contributed to the accident.'

I looked at the clock. It was 8.30 p.m. The crash had happened not long before I had tried Anita's number. Anita had likely been on her way to the TV studio when she was killed.

I kept thinking of Anita that night and tossed and turned more than I slept. Zoya had never met Anita but had heard so much about her from me that she also looked ashen when we parted ways in the morning for work. Aman seemed to sense my mood. When I strapped him into his booster seat on the way to drop him at preschool, he looked at me with wide eyes, his eyes asking the question that perhaps he couldn't yet put into words. Was I okay? Finally, his lips began quivering and he was about to cry, perhaps sensing just how tense I was.

I tousled his hair. 'It's okay, sweetheart. Someone Daddy knew is…not well.'

He just looked at me and smiled when I forced myself to smile at him.

'Dada, okay?'

I nodded and smiled. How did one explain death to such a young child? I clearly had much to learn when it came to be a father. We drove to his preschool, and I popped in his latest favourite CD. Listening to nursery rhymes with Aman giggling along did a bit to improve my mood, but as soon as I pulled into his school and dropped him off to his class, my smile disappeared.

I had not wanted to spook Aman, but from the time we had left home, I'd had a feeling we were not alone. Seeing the black Honda City parked a few metres away confirmed those suspicions. That same car had been following us since I had turned out of our society gates.

I left my car and walked down towards Central Avenue at a brisk pace and then turned left, breaking into a sprint. I cut through an adjoining housing society, whose guard gaped at me as I ran past him, jumped a wall, and soon was behind the black car. I realized a couple of things in those few seconds. Whoever my shadow was, he was not a professional. He had let me disappear from sight, which made little sense if he had indeed been following me. But he had remained parked outside the school after following me soon after I left home, and I had not seen any child with him, so he was not a parent who had come to drop off his child. I stayed there watching as he got out of his car and ambled over to the gate, chatting with the guard. He was lean and was wearing a neatly pressed suit. He could easily have passed for a young professional who had come to check this school before seeking admission for his child or perhaps come by to meet a teacher. Was I just being paranoid? Maybe he was nothing more than an ordinary father. Maybe I was overreacting. I gave him that benefit of the doubt for only a few more seconds as I circled around his car and flattened myself against a wall just a few metres from him.

I could now hear what he was saying.

'I'm Aman Ghosh's uncle. His mother sent me. His father just dropped him off but forgot to send his tiffin along. I was passing by and she asked me to give it to him. Could I please meet him?'

I closed my eyes, telling myself to calm down. Whoever this man was, he had come not for me, but for my son. I had thought I could create a new life where I could shelter Zoya and Aman from the world I had seen. Hearing this man made me realize that had been a futile hope. I had no idea what he wanted or why he wanted to get to Aman, but it didn't matter. If he thought he could hurt my son, he had no idea who he was dealing with. I was many things—a father, a husband, an executive—but deep down, I was a man with certain unique skills the government had spent a lot of time, money and effort drumming into me. Part of that training was that when faced with an imminent threat, there was no better course of action than to be direct, brutal and decisive.

The guard went into check on what he should do, and I stepped behind the man in the suit. He began to turn his head hearing me approach, but he was too late. My left hand snaked around his neck, while my right went around his head in the opposite direction. He croaked in anguish as I pressed down on his jugular.

'I could just keep the pressure on, and you will suffocate to death. Slow and painful. Or I could put sudden pressure and snap your jugular. Much faster but you'll feel some pain. Of course, I could just adjust my grip and snap to one side and break your neck. So many ways to kill you. Which would you prefer? Quick or slow? Painful or painless?'

He just gurgled, though his body went limp, indicating that resistance wasn't exactly on his mind. I dragged him into the adjoining alley and then, remembering that he had been stalking my little son, threw him over my hip. He hit the rough pavement hard, his breath coming out of him in a giant and audible 'whoosh' as if he were a punctured balloon. He put his right hand in his pocket and before he could complete his action, I had my blade against his neck.

'This is a Victorinox Ranger Grip 178. An ordinary Swiss Army knife to the uninitiated. Serves well to cut through rope or vines. But it does just fine at cutting through a human neck. Believe me, I know it works. I've done it before.'

He squealed, his voice a hoarse whisper. 'Just taking out my card.'

I took a look at the business card he produced. So, my chap was Nishant Sinha, a private investigator.

'Who sent you?'

'The board of school trustees wanted to test security protocol. They just paid me to check if someone could ask to talk to the children without proper verification.'

'Why the fuck were you following me and why did you ask for my son by name?'

His eyes showed genuine surprise. 'They showed me a consent form you had signed.'

I let go of him, though I kept his card and pocketed my knife. I pulled him to his feet.

'I now know who you are and where you work. Spread the word among your fellow investigators. Snooping around me or my family is going to be very bad for their health. Now, I'll take you along to the police for a little chat.'

The mention of the police spurred him to some resistance, and he tried to push me away. Not a very smart idea. I slapped him, sending him spinning against the wall. As he tried to recover his balance, I punched him in the gut and he went down, wheezing and sputtering.

'You do not want to fuck with me. Understand?'

His eyes were bulging in terror and he just nodded. As I walked back to my car, hauling him behind me, I could feel my heart pounding. It wasn't from the adrenaline rush of the little incident that had just transpired. It came from knowing that my family was in danger.

'Congratulations on the additional star,' I said. 'First time we've met since you got promoted.'

Ashutosh Phadke looked at me with his usual smile, his eyes twinkling. 'You created all the mayhem, I just cleaned it up. Not a bad reward for playing the role of a clean-up crew.'

Phadke had been the officer who had once arrested me. He was a good man, a friend and, above all, an honest officer. Which was why I had come to him directly versus going through the regular police bureaucracy. He had recently been promoted to Deputy Inspector General and, given his track record, he was already being spoken of as someone who could one day be the Commissioner of Police for Mumbai. In short, a very good friend to have at a time like this.

Phadke pointed to the sullen and bruised investigator I had hauled in. 'He's an idiot, but his story checks out. He was indeed contacted for this job and the buffoon took it without even asking for a face-to-face meeting or authenticating his client.'

Sinha cringed and shrank back in his chair, wondering what else was in store for him after the beating I had given him.

Phadke glared at him. 'Get out and if I hear a single complaint about you again, I will make sure you go out of business.'

As Sinha walked out, Phadke turned to me, his eyes all business now that we were alone. 'I checked with the trustees of the school. They know nothing about this guy. Looks like someone hacked their email to send the message to this joker and later spoke with him on the phone to brief him. They also sent a consent letter that had your forged signature. Not a particularly good forgery, but Sinha wouldn't have known any better. Aadi, you have made many enemies—jihadis, local thugs, in Afghanistan and who knows who else. The offer of police protection is still open. After what you did, the home minister himself asked me if you wanted protection if some jihadi came looking for revenge.'

I had not wanted Zoya or Aman to live under the shadow of a threat, but it felt like I had few good options. I just nodded and went straight to Zoya's office. She was safe while she was in office, but she did go out for lunch today and I wanted to be sure she was okay.

I had already called in sick at work, and, still numbed by the news of Anita's death, Randhawa had perhaps not even registered much of what I said.

Zoya's eyes sparkled with surprise as she saw me outside her office building. 'What happened?'

'Nothing. Just thought we could have a lunch date.'

She looked sceptical but grabbed my hand and soon we were sitting at Aromas, which was a short walk from her workplace. When I told her what had happened at Aman's school, she grabbed her bag. 'Let's go get him.'

'I already took care of that. He's with Ravi and Rekha. From tomorrow, there will be a policeman outside his school…and one who will accompany you to work.'

Anger blazed in her eyes for a second before she made an effort to suppress it. I knew what was going through her mind. That her baby was in danger and perhaps I was responsible. The moment passed, but in that second, I saw what being a mother really did to a woman, what it did to her priorities.

I held her hand. 'Zo, I don't know who put that investigator up to this, and I have no idea if they'll try anything again, but I can promise you nobody will ever hurt Aman or you while I'm there.'

Even as I said those words, I wondered if I could live up to that promise.

Ravi was looking at me over the glass of wine in front of him, no doubt waiting for when we'd be alone so he could tell me what was on his mind. When Rekha and Zoya went inside with Aman, he raised his glass in a toast. 'To the unfortunate bastards who think they can hunt you.'

I touched my glass to his. A few years ago, I would have been pleased at the toast. But now, I did not want anyone to hunt me or for me to have to hunt them back.

Ravi must have seen the expression on my face. 'If it is a local behind this, it's someone much more subtle than the usual lot. If one of usual suspects really wanted to come for you, they would come for you straight out, not hack emails and so on. We've tangled with enough of them. They are many things, but subtle isn't one of them.'

'Then who?'

'No idea, my boy. But these are pros. Someone who has had much more training than the average chap. They didn't send this clown of an investigator to cause any harm to Aman, but to check for vulnerabilities, to see if getting to Aman can be a way to get to you. You can be sure they're watching other aspects of your life. I don't know who these guys are, but if they know your background, they may well have set this idiot to send you a message. A message that they know who you are and who matters to you and that if they want, they can get to them. I don't know about you, but I don't believe that whole Operation Lotus began and ended with that American Ross whom you put out of business in Afghanistan. And the pot you stirred has a lot of nasty characters—jihadis, drug smugglers, private military contractors, Chinese special forces. Characters who know enough to not come after you, but to look for other softer targets around you.'

I didn't say anything, but I knew what he meant. Zoya and Aman.

My phone rang. It was Phadke.

'Aadi, I checked. The IB guys haven't picked up any chatter on jihadi channels, so they don't think one of your old friends was behind this, but you never know. Be careful.'

When we got home, I could see a policeman already there, chatting with the security guard.

I stopped to shake his hand. 'Thank you for being here.'

He stood straight and saluted. 'Constable Ram on duty, sir. I haven't seen anything out of the ordinary in the time I have been here.'

Aman giggled and tried to salute back, at which the cop beamed at him.

'Sir, you can be sure nobody will harm your family while I'm here.'

I liked the open, honest smile on his face, and I smiled back. I exchanged numbers with him, and I asked him to drop by if he wanted water or tea. A part of me wondered how he would fare with his slight paunch, likely lack of anything but basic firearms training, and his antiquated .303 rifle if men with AK-47s came for me and my family. For that matter, how would I fare? I had my training, I had the motivation to protect my family, but the bottom line was that, armed with nothing more than a knife, I wouldn't last long or do much to protect my family if they were attacked.

Zoya caught the look on my face as we walked to the lift lobby. 'Aadi, you okay? You seem lost somewhere.'

'I'm fine.'

Actually, I wasn't. I was putting myself in the shoes of an attacker, and I could already see how easy it would be to take me and my family out. A single trained attacker could kill the elderly security guard and the policeman without much fuss. A team of four could get to our apartment in minutes, perhaps two in the elevator and two coming up the stairs to block any escape. Kick in or shoot open the main door. They would incapacitate me first. If they wanted to toy with me later, a burst to the legs would put me down. I closed my eyes, not even willing to think of what might happen to Zoya and Aman if I was not able to protect them.

As we went upstairs, I asked Zoya to stand back while I approached the door.

'Aadi, now you're scaring me.'

I didn't say anything, but we were right to be scared. Before leaving, I had attached a small piece of Scotch tape to the door hinge, a trick I had picked up from an intelligence operative who had once trained with us. The idea was simple—if someone had come calling while you were out and opened the door, the tape would show signs of being displaced. In this case, it was much worse. The tape wasn't there. In its place was a thick piece of red tape, exactly where I had placed my tape but with a smiley drawn on it with a black marker. Someone had been here all right, and it wasn't a bumbling investigator like Sinha. It was a pro, who had walked through the gate, past the policeman and guard, seen through my precautions, perhaps laughed at my attempts at playing spy and left his own message for me.

The question was: What was the message?

Was it a warning that they would come for me later? If they had made it so far, they would have waited for an ambush, not left a clever message and gone away.

As I reached for the door handle, I froze. Who was I dealing with here? As I took a closer look, the red tape's edge was off the door, indicating that whoever had placed it had either not pressed it shut, or perhaps the people who had placed it had opened the door after placing it. Perhaps waiting for me to lower my guard, thinking the intruder had left after messing with the tape outside. Or perhaps they had gone back in to check something after leaving the tape. Either way, they could still be inside our home.

I reached into my pocket to get my phone to call Phadke when the door swung open. It was not pulled open fast as if someone inside was trying to rush out but leisurely as if the people inside were leaving, oblivious to the fact that we were outside.

In the darkness of our apartment inside, I couldn't see

how many were waiting or whether they were armed, but I didn't wait. I rocked back and kicked the door as hard as I could, putting all my weight into that one kick. The door slammed into whoever was inside and I heard a shout of pain.

I could hear Zoya screaming behind me, but I was focused only on what lay ahead. I blinked rapidly, trying to get my eyes adjusted quicker to the darkness while the men inside, taken totally by surprise, hesitated.

A second was all I needed. I had my knife out in my right hand and my car keys lodged between the knuckles of my left, and I stepped in towards them, slashing high with my left towards a face and slashing low with my right towards where the midsection would be. The man screamed and fell back. I took another step forward and to the right, this time reversing the strike, slashing backhanded with my left and then following with a lunge towards an exposed neck.

The action had lasted only a couple of seconds, but I knew when to back off. There might be several men inside who could overpower me; one or more of them might have guns. Too many ways for me to get into a losing battle if I stayed and fought. I had the initiative and I had to use that advantage to get my family out of harm's way.

As I reached the door, I pulled it shut and then ran back to where Zoya stood, frozen in shock, her arms around Aman. 'Down the stairs! Now!'

As we raced down, I called the constable. 'Ram, we're under attack! Coming down the stairs.'

I heard the door slam open behind us, but I wasn't going to be distracted by who was pursuing us. I had Aman in one arm and Zoya was in front of me. We were just one floor away when Ram Singh came up, his rifle at the ready.

As we stopped near him, we could hear heavy boots following us. Ram's eyes widened as they met mine. 'Sir, you go down with your family. I'll hold them.'

I heard the unmistakable sound of a round being chambered in an automatic pistol, and then repeated. Two men with pistols, perhaps others with them. Ram Singh's hands were shaking but he had his rifle up at his shoulder. No, I would not have this good man die saving me. I took the rifle from him and handed Aman to him.

'Take my family down.'

We continued climbing down the stairwell, our pursuers not far behind. I spotted a portable fire extinguisher to a side of the stairwell, kicked open the glass casing that shielded it and pulled it out. As I saw the outline of the first man round the corner at the top of the stairwell, I tossed it towards him. The extinguisher landed at his feet and I shot it.

The Enfield 0.303 is a venerable weapon, its first ancestor being used as far back as 1895. While its rate of fire makes it no match for modern automatic weapons, its stopping power at close range is to be feared, something that its adversaries have learned the hard way, starting with Zulus who first encountered it in British hands to Russian soldiers who faced it in the hands of mujahideen in Afghanistan.

At less than ten feet away, the bullet punched through the fire extinguisher, and it exploded in a burst of white smoke. The first man stumbled in confusion and came sprawling down the stairs. I slammed the heavy stock of the Enfield against his head, solid Indian rosewood machined at the Ishapore arms factory ending what gravity had started.

The man crashed to one side, stunned. The second man was now coming through the smoke and I ran down the stairs, not waiting to engage him in a close-quarters gunfight when his automatic pistol could put out many, many more rounds in a short period of time than I could hope to with the old rifle.

As I reached the ground floor, I could see Ram Singh and the guard near the gate, with Zoya and Aman behind him. I ran to the left, not wanting them in the line of fire if the man behind me shot at me. I knelt behind a parked car and aimed the rifle at the stairs, waiting for my attacker to show himself.

He never did. He must have sensed he was being lured into an ambush and as we waited, we heard the wails of police sirens approaching. Someone had no doubt called the cops with the gunshot and the shouting in the building.

As the first police car stopped near the gate and three armed policemen ran out, I dropped the rifle, not wanting to be shot in the confusion, and called Phadke. The policemen saw the rifle near me and trained their guns on me, screaming at me to put my hands up. Once again, I was taken into custody by the Mumbai Police, mistaken for a terrorist.

'You need to disappear for a while, or at least get your family to disappear.'

Phadke had been all business when he'd strode into his office last night, shouting orders at his men to release me and screaming to ask which idiot constable had been on guard duty at our apartment. I did not envy Ram Singh the chewing out he would no doubt get for letting the intruders in. Once Phadke had cleared up with the cops who I was, we'd been whisked away to a police guest house where we'd spent the night. Aman, with the resilience and innocence of the truly young, had managed to fall asleep almost immediately, but Zoya and I had not slept a minute. Phadke's men had been through our apartment all night, trying to make sense of what had happened, and looking at his bloodshot eyes, I knew he had perhaps spent much of the night up with them.

'What did you find?'

Phadke sat down opposite me with a loud sigh. 'God knows who's after you and why. Both men were gone by the time our guys got up the stairs, and if you knocked one out, he's either pretty tough or his friend got him out. Either way, they acted like trained professionals. They got in through a rear gate that is used by the deliverymen, a gate that is guarded at all times of day except thirty minutes each evening when the guards rotate. They knew that and had planned for it. That tells me they were watching your place for at least a couple of days, to get the pattern right. As you said, they saw through your tape trick. They were wearing gloves and we found no prints.'

I had known Phadke for over two years and we had seen a lot together, but I had rarely seen him this worried. 'The funny thing is that I don't think they had come to kill you. You surprised them, when they were on their way out. If they had wanted to kill you, they could have just waited inside and not opened the door. You were lucky.'

'Ashutosh, why were they there? All along, I had assumed some jihadi wannabes remembered me from one of their damn kill lists and came after me to make a name for themselves. But if they weren't there to just kill me, why were they there?'

That was when Phadke shrugged helplessly. 'I've had my best detectives looking at your home. Whoever these guys were, they weren't just there, lying in wait for you; they were looking for something. They opened all the cupboards, drawers and desks. My men printed those, and saw your and Zoya's fingerprints smudged over, as if someone wearing gloves had opened and closed them.'

I thought through the inescapable conclusion that Phadke gave voice to.

'They were looking for something. But what? Your study seems to have been the most worked over, with the bookshelves seemingly all rifled through. Have a look.' He showed me photos of the bookshelves on his phone, and I froze at one photo.

All the books were there, but a corner of the bookshelf was empty. That was where I used to keep old papers—bank statements, income tax receipts, rent agreements and the like—in a couple of boxes. All those papers were strewn across the floor.

I thought of Anita Padmanabhan, of the paper she'd so desperately wanted me to look at. Of intruders in her house, threatening her, following her, leaving a dead cat on her doorstep. All things I had taken to be paranoia or stress. Of her being convinced that her phone was being tapped. I had refused to listen to her or help her. Suddenly I wasn't so sure anymore that she had indeed died in an accident.

I slammed my hand down on the desk in frustration. If her phone had indeed been tapped, whoever was doing it would have heard her talking to me, telling me about the paper she supposedly had been given. What was in this paper that made some people go to such lengths to find it? By refusing to help Anita, I had lost my chance at knowing what it was. And now, even if I had no idea what it was, those trying to get it back were hunting me, thinking I knew more about it than I did. And I was going in blind.

That afternoon, Ravi and Rekha came to meet us at the guest house. I had gone with the cops to get some of our clothes and belongings and also used the opportunity to get some of Aman's toys. He was busy playing with them in a corner of the living room while Rekha asked the question that was on all our minds.

'When can you go back home?'

The short answer was that we had no idea. I couldn't contemplate going back there till we knew who was after me and what they wanted. After what had happened, both Zoya and I had concluded that there was no question of her going to work or Aman going to school either. Our lives had been placed on hold, and my hatred for those unknown men behind this grew with each passing moment.

Phadke came by later in the evening, holding a thick folder. He sat with us for some time, chatting and then nodded at me, looking towards Aman. I got the hint.

'Zo, how about we get Aman settled on the bed inside and put some cartoons on TV?'

Aman reacted with glee as he heard the magic word 'cartoons' and, after Zoya had him settled, we gathered around Phadke. He looked around once, asking me if he could share what he had with Ravi and Rekha around.

'They're family and they've been through a lot with us. So they can hear anything we can.'

He laid the folder on the table in front of him. 'I've had our labs and detectives working overtime. We cannot have goons on the loose, attacking people in their homes again.'

'What did they find?'

He pointed to the folder. 'Depends on how you look at it. One could say they found a fair bit, but then again, one could say they've not found the most important thing we need to know.'

He pointed to one chart. 'Blood can tell all sorts of interesting things, and whoever they were, you made them both bleed.'

I had seen the blood on my keys and knife, but it was nice to know that I had hurt the bastards who had violated the sanctuary of my home.

'We got two distinct blood samples and in sufficient quantities to show that you caused them both some serious pain. As I said, geeks can read all kinds of things in the blood. One thing that they can read is what they call a person's biological age, and our geeks say that chances are that these men were somewhere in the late twenties or early thirties.'

'They can tell someone's age from a blood sample?'

Phadke looked at Zoya and smiled. 'Not entirely, but from the proteins in the sample, they can estimate what they call the biological age. So, someone who takes poor care of their body through smoking or drinking will show up with a biological age higher than their real age. In this case, from all we gather, we had two fit, young men who probably took good care of their bodies.'

I didn't need a blood test to tell me that. Most professionals at the top of their game in this line of work would be in their late twenties or early thirties. Old enough to have learned the ropes, and young enough to not lose the reflexes and fitness of youth. I didn't say that to Phadke, though. I needed to know everything he had learned without trying to be a smartass.

'There's something else…'

Ravi suddenly put up his hand, apologizing to Phadke for the interruption, as he turned on the volume of the TV set in the living room where we were seated. Varsha Singh was on screen as the images behind her showed the flags of China and India crossing each other, with two rifles on top of them.

'Reports are coming in from the northern border about a gun battle involving Indian and Chinese troops. While details are sketchy, we are hearing that a Chinese patrol, when challenged by Indian troops, opened fire. The Indian army returned fire and the gun battle lasted for a few minutes before commanders on both sides stopped the fighting. There are no reports of confirmed casualties on either side at this stage. We will keep you updated with more…'

'Before long, the bloody Chinese will want to provoke another fight. I don't think they can deal with the fact that finally we're standing up to their bullying,' Ravi said.

I let him rant for a bit, but while what had happened along the border concerned me, my bigger concerns were far more immediate. As we muted the TV, I asked Phadke what else he had found.

'Blood tests also show how often and to what level of severity the person has suffered from colds. I can't pretend to understand the science, but something to do with antibodies in the blood. The lab techs tell me that one of these men had a very high frequency of cold exposure and also built up much higher immunity to it than the other.'

'What does that mean?'

Phadke caught the hint of irritation in my voice. 'As I said, these bloody techies can only tell us so much, not who these men were or who sent them. But what this particular fact means, according to them, is that one of them had a profile consistent with someone who lives in temperate places like Mumbai. Perhaps a local, though that's far from sure. He could have lived in any number of places with similar climate. The other guy, however, according to them, could have spent a lot of time in much colder climates, such as in the extreme north of India, or from another colder clime. Also, he seems to have been injected with antibodies to protect against yellow fever and Ebola. Normally you'd get those while travelling to Africa. That makes for a very curious kind of background.'

Ravi and I exchanged a look. A Chinese special forces officer who had served in shitholes around the world would likely have been in Africa, where China had been expanding its presence aggressively. I sat back, thinking of Anita Padmanabhan in a cell, guarded by so-called pirates many of whom were almost certainly Chinese soldiers; of my old Chinese pal from the Korengal Valley who had suddenly showed up in the guise of a pirate; of the men who had hunted her and now perhaps turned on me; of the paper Anita had found there that had perhaps led to her death.

I had a feeling that I knew who one of the men who had been at my home was.

'Sir, are you coming to the office?'

The call from the office mailroom was a surprise since I had already called Randhawa and told him I wouldn't be in. I hadn't given him all the gory details, but the morning newspapers were full of reports of how a shooting had erupted in a housing society near Powai and speculation as to whether terrorists were behind it. Some idiot of a neighbour had mentioned to reporters that I was involved and, much to my irritation, my name was back in the news for all the wrong reasons yet again, acting like a magnet for whichever wacko jihadi-wannabe out there who may want to win his laurels.

'No, I'm not well, so I have the day off.'

'Okay, sir. There's an envelope for you. Anita…'

I cut him off immediately. 'Got to go. I don't have time to talk. Will check in later.'

He sounded puzzled, even hurt, but what I had taken to be Anita's paranoia was something I needed to embrace if I was to stay a step ahead of those after me. She had suspected her phone had been tapped, and that was how they had decided on coming after me. As I put my phone in my pocket, I wondered if they were tapping mine too. Whoever these guys were, they had demonstrated that they were pros. Assuming they were unlikely to keep tabs on all potential sources of Anita's contact would be one of the costliest mistakes I could make.

I picked up the landline at the guest house and called the peon back. 'It's me. Now talk.'

'Anita madam had come by a couple of days ago and left an envelope that she said I should give only to you.'

I could feel my breathing stop for a second as I processed what he said.

'When did she come by?'

'In the evening, sir. Maybe around seven.'

That would have been around the time she had been on her way to the television station. That would also have been just before she had died in what I was no longer sure was an accident.

'Keep it. I'm coming over now.' I thought it over, then added, 'On second thoughts, no. Here is a landline number. Write it down. Can you ask Randhawa sir to call me on it from a landline? That's important. Ask him not to call from his mobile but to use a landline that is not his office number.'

A few minutes later, the phone rang. Randhawa. He sounded tired. The death of one of his employees and the attack on me was taking its toll on him.

'Aadi, what's with the cloak-and-dagger stuff?'

'Sir, can we meet for a cup of coffee? There's a package the mailroom guy has. Can you get it and bring it with you?'

'I was coming down with a flu, so thought I'd take the rest of the day off. I'll pass by Powai as I head home, so sure, let's catch up.'

'Sir, let's meet up where I met you for our first interview.'

'Sure, where...'

I cut him off again. I couldn't take the risk that the office phones had also been tapped. Just a few days ago, I had ignored Anita's pleas for help, thinking she was losing her mind. Now, I was in the same shoes as her.

'Sir, let's meet up soon. Tangos could be nearby, exercise caution.'

By the time I reached Renaissance Hotel in Powai, Zoya had sent me four messages asking if I was okay. She had shouted at me when I left and I had told her I needed to go for something urgent and would be back soon. One constable had tagged along and sat beside me, wondering whether I had lost my mind as I drove like a maniac to get to the hotel.

When I reached the coffee shop, I scanned the room for Randhawa and missed him at first. Then I grinned. The old sailor had done his bit. His usual bright turban was gone. He was wearing a cap, with tinted glasses over his eyes.

As I sat opposite him, he took off his glasses and winked. 'So, my boy, you've got me playing James Bond at my age. What's that about tangos? I suspected you were trying to conceal yourself from some of your jihadi buddies, so I took precautions. And you stroll in casually and I feel like a foolish old man pretending to be a secret agent or something.'

I smiled. I had bet on him reacting to the word we in the forces would use for enemies.

'The package, sir?'

'Oh, yes, here.'

He slipped a small brown envelope the size of a paperback to me. I felt it between my fingers, wondering if this was the paper Anita had mentioned. It dawned on me that she had been followed and was sure she would never make it to the TV station, and had left it for me as a desperate last measure, hoping I would do something with it. What was in this envelope to have caused so much havoc already? And more importantly, now that I had it with me, how much more was to follow?

'Sir, did the peon say anything about what happened when Anita left this for me?'

I could see the sorrow in his eyes as he answered. 'You know, he was puzzled because Anita came in with two identical-looking envelopes. She left one for you and took one with her.'

Anita had been tough and smart. Anyone pursuing her wouldn't know she had dropped off something at the office. Had the police got an envelope from the accident site? I filed that away as something I'd ask Phadke.

I drove back to the guest house, hoping I was not being followed and barely able to contain my curiosity. When I got back, I got thoroughly chewed out by Zoya. 'What the hell were you thinking? Rushing off with one constable?'

I pulled her into my arms.

'Zo, nobody knows where we are. I was as careful as I could be, but it was very important that I go.' I held the envelope out towards her. 'This has the paper Anita had spoken about. The paper that got her killed and led to those men to our house.'

I saw the gleam in her eyes and knew that she was just as curious to see what was in it. After putting Aman to bed, we opened the envelope. Inside it was a plain-looking paper, frayed at the edges, with what looked like a list scrawled in Chinese. I couldn't make head or tails of what was written there, but as I turned the paper, I froze, looking at what was on it.

There was a word on it. A single word.

Invictus.

Below that was a symbol, seemingly made with someone's fingers, drawn in the same rust-brown colour—drawn with blood. A symbol I knew only too well, a symbol that had defined my identity for years.

Anita was right. This paper and the message on it needed to get to the right people.

—➤—

We barely ate dinner. We could see Aman was puzzled at the sombre mood in the room. He had woken up, cranky that we had not been paying him any attention. To compensate, we had ordered in some ice cream. That had mollified him, along with the fact that he got to watch cartoons non-stop for hours while we chatted. Finally, when he was tucked in, Zoya turned to me and I could see the haunted expression on her face.

'Aadi, what do we do?'

Now that Aman was asleep, I felt myself sagging, coming to grips with what I had seen. I sat down heavily on a chair and could feel tears start to form in my eyes. 'It's my fault. She's dead because I didn't believe her. She's dead because I didn't do anything to help her.'

Zoya held me close. 'If you had blundered in without knowing what we were dealing with, we might all be dead.'

I held her, knowing that in her own way, Zoya was right. She had a family now, and her instinct to protect our family, even if it led to hard choices, was right. However, that was a choice that I found hard to live with, knowing that it might have led to Anita's death. Before I could say anything more, my mobile rang.

It was Randhawa, and he sounded distraught. 'Aadi, when I came home, I noticed a voice mail on my phone. I had ignored it because it was from an unfamiliar number. Thank God I listened to it. It was from Anita the evening she died. She said she had tried me on my mobile but couldn't get through. Aadi, she called to say goodbye. She said some men were after her. That she had something they wanted. She thanked me for everything I had done for her.'

He broke down. My heart was pounding. Randhawa had no idea how much danger he had put himself in by calling me and talking about Anita. Anyone listening in would wonder what else she had told him.

'Sir, we will talk some other time. I'll call you back.'

'What are you saying, Aadi?'

I disconnected and called back from the landline. I wasn't sure if I should tell him about the paper. The more he knew, the more the danger he could be in.

'Sir, be careful. I am not sure how all these things are connected, but the incident at my home, Anita's death, could all have been executed by the same people. Do you want me to put you in touch with the cops? They could keep you safe till things are sorted out.'

He was silent, perhaps shocked at what he was hearing. 'You mean Anita's death wasn't an accident?'

'I can't be sure, sir, but I think she was killed.'

'Why?'

'Sir, we don't have time. You need to get away from your home and to safety.'

I heard him sigh.

'Aadi, my wife passed away a few years ago. I live with a bed-ridden mother who is ninety and can't be moved without a wheelchair. I have arthritis and need four pills a day to keep going with my diabetes and kidney problems. Do you think I'm going to run off?'

'Sir, I'm calling the police. They will be there soon.'

As I put the phone down, I wondered how much Randhawa believed that lie. I told Phadke some jihadis had threatened Randhawa because of his association with me and I was worried about his safety. Zoya and I sat at the table, the landline and my mobile on it, waiting to hear back. Finally, I couldn't bear it and called Randhawa after half an hour.

'Sir, have the cops arrived?'

'No, son. Not yet.' His voice sounded calm. As he spoke, my heart broke as I realized the old soldier knew what was coming. 'I hugged and kissed my mother, watered my plants and drank a glass of good Scotch. My boy, I have no regrets, and have nothing to be ashamed of. You're a good man, and you…'

I heard the doorbell ringing and hoped it was the cops.

'Aadi, give me a minute. Maybe the cops are here.'

Randhawa must have kept the mobile in his hands as I heard him walk towards the door and open it. 'Who are you?'

Then I heard the unmistakable sound of gunshots. Two of them in quick succession. I heard someone's breathing as he picked up the phone, perhaps surprised there was an active call. Then, silence.

Two days later, I was at Randhawa's funeral. His son had flown over from the US and I could see that my boss had commanded the kind of loyalty and affection that only the best of officers did. He had left the armed forces several years ago, but dozens of his old colleagues and men were there, paying homage. In fact, the funeral appeared to be filled with people wearing uniforms.

Phadke had initially balked at my going to the funeral, but when I insisted, he had in turn insisted on sending with me a large contingent of armed policemen. Before Randhawa's body was consigned to the flames, I walked up to him, seeing his serene face obscured in part by a bandage which, from what Phadke had told me, concealed the bullet wound to the head that had killed him. A second shot had entered and passed through his abdomen.

'I'm sorry, boss. I'm so sorry. I never thought you would lose your life because of me.'

Another good man dead. Because I had so wanted to lead a safe and cloistered life that I had ignored Anita's pleas for help. I closed my eyes and swore. Anita, Randhawa, both gone. Was it my curse that I was to be left alive while good men and women around me died?

A thought came to my mind. No, it was not a curse. It was a responsibility. A responsibility to ensure that their deaths had not been in vain.

'Boss, I will make them pay. Whoever did this will pay.'

My eyes were glistening and I never realized how loudly I had spoken or that there was a man standing next to me, listening to it all. He coughed gently and I turned and looked into the eyes of a man I had last met when I had been in an army hospital after the events in Afghanistan a year earlier.

Maloy Krishna Dhar, a spymaster who had retired as Joint Director of the Intelligence Bureau, only to reinvent himself as a bestselling author. His views on security and willingness to speak his mind had led me to reach out to him during the Mumbai attacks. Then he had come through for me when I had been deep in enemy territory in Afghanistan, trying to rescue Zoya and Aman. I knew that I was alive thanks in large measure to the strings Dhar had pulled. Randhawa had told me that an old friend had strongly recommended me for the job, and seeing Dhar here confirmed my suspicions about who that old friend was.

He averted his eyes and walked past me to pay his last respects.

As he passed me, he whispered under his breath. 'Five o'clock. Screen 6 in the multiplex at R-City. I'll find you.'

The old spymaster had certainly not forgotten me, and I was glad he hadn't. Once more, I found myself and those I cared about in danger and I could do with his advice.

The movie playing at that time was a Bollywood tearjerker I would never have come to watch. I smiled, reminding myself that I would never have come to such a movie when I had been single. With Zoya, I would have come to many such movies just to be with her. The smile disappeared when I recalled I had been in this very mall with her when a man in front of us had been shot almost three years ago.

I checked my watch. Five past five and no sign of Dhar. I was about to get up when an elderly Sikh gentleman walked past me, leaning on his cane, and sat next to me.

'Thank you for giving an old spy a chance to get up to his old tricks again.' I sat up with a jolt, nearly spilling some of the Coke that was in my hand as he continued. 'Don't look at me. Just chat. Tell me why my friend was killed.'

I spoke for ten minutes in a low whisper and he listened, interrupting me only once or twice for clarifications.

'Do you want to see a copy of the paper? I have the original in a safe place.'

'No. If some hard, young men get very persuasive with me and ask if I've seen it, it's better if I can truthfully say I've never. Hanging on to some sliver of truth is always good to survive torture.'

He said it without a trace of amusement, and I wondered what would get such a seasoned officer to fear such an outcome. 'Is it the Chinese? Are they trying to close down everyone who knows about the paper? Why did nobody in our government react when Anita told them about it?'

He shook his head slowly. 'First, as to why nobody in the government reacted to what Anita shared, I really don't know. Could be usual bureaucratic apathy, or if you want to get really paranoid, assume our Chinese friends have infiltrated some of our channels and blocked this message from getting to the people who might have cared. As for who? I doubt it's the Chinese government, at least not directly. Governments don't do this stuff in each other's backyards all that often. You've seen the news, haven't you? Indian and Chinese troops are facing off each day, and everyone's wondering if there will be a war. Why would they start killing people in India, and risk creating a bigger international incident?'

'Who else?'

He was silent, as if thinking it over. 'Let's review the facts. They are certainly tapping phones. That's how they knew about Anita contacting you and going to the TV station. Also, they must have tapped Randhawa's number so they knew to go after him. They have demonstrated the ability to hack mails, and are getting killings done by professionals. My guess is you're dealing with the one thing worse than a government up to dirty tricks.'

He paused to sip the cup of coffee he had in his hand before continuing. 'Non-state actors, as we call them, with the resources or tacit backing of some elements of the government. That means they have many of the capabilities a state agency would, but don't need to act with the discretion a government would, since they are not tied down by any niceties. In short, I suspect someone in the Chinese establishment, with or without knowledge of their senior leadership, has a few secrets to hide. If I throw in your Chinese friend from Afghanistan, then certainly he's not just a gun for hire working for a private agency, but is very much, directly or indirectly, being used by some government agency.'

I digested it all. I was looking at the screen, but nothing unfolding there really registered. What could I possibly do to protect those I loved against an enemy like this? Should I go to Phadke and tell him everything?

Dhar seemed to have read my mind. 'Don't go to the cops, not with this. Your family should be safe. They have already been given police protection. Whoever is orchestrating this preferred to cover their tracks by making it look like accidents or robberies. The official story on Randhawa is a botched robbery. The bastards left his mother alive and cleaned up all the money to make it look so. I doubt they will go after your family.'

He paused, as if thinking it over. 'But you never know. So get your family extra protection. You've done enough favours to the government to cash in on some. The operation in Afghanistan got the Indian government many brownie points with the US. They didn't have anything to do with it, but they did bask in your reflected glory.'

'But...'

He chuckled. 'Yes, yes, I know you don't want any glory, but do you really think our political masters will pass on a chance to get some leverage against Pakistan? They may have implied to the US that you were working under their direction. So the Americans owe us big time.'

I shook my head, disgusted at how things never really changed. People like me went into harm's way and politicians sat in their air-conditioned rooms and used us.

'I'm just an old man, but the prime minister himself told the new IB director that we all owed a debt of gratitude to whoever had helped unmask that conspiracy in Mumbai and then for what happened in Korengal. You don't need to do anything. I can just nudge a few old friends and many things can happen. Once our leadership knows what's in this paper and what it has unleashed, given your history, they will ensure that they look out for you. You won't have to guess when someone is coming to kill your family. But remember, once I make those calls, you are no longer an anonymous civilian at a desk job. You're taking sides in what is for all intents and purposes a shooting war. Up for that, Major?'

I just nodded. There wasn't much to think about. I had taken sides the moment Anita and Randhawa had been killed and my family threatened.

When the government is bogged down by its natural lethargy, it can move so slowly as to make you want to tear your hair out. That is something most Indians have experienced at some point or another and often take for granted. But when it wants to move, it is able to cut through the usual political or bureaucratic bullshit. When that agenda is pushed from the top, it can move at incredible speed and do some amazing things. I guess that is the little-known secret of how the Indian armed forces are able to do what they do without getting mired in a lot of the issues their civilian counterparts face.

I got a glimpse of that the next evening when six heavily armed men wearing black uniforms stood in front of the guest house. They all served with the elite National Security Guards and as I walked out to meet them, they all stood at attention and saluted. It was a bit embarrassing, and the three policemen whom Phadke had put on guard were staring, looking both uncomfortable and inadequate. But I'll be honest, part of me felt good about being in the company of such men again.

Their leader stepped forward. 'Sir, Naik Ramarao Gaikwad reporting.'

I nodded at him and got the names of all the other men. Then I asked where they were from and also asked them about their families. An old habit that came back naturally to me. A good officer knows each and every one of his men. They are never faceless and nameless grunts. Men who would gladly lay down their lives for you deserve that much respect.

'Gaikwad, you and your men are among the finest in the country, and you'll be here protecting my family, which is perhaps not the kind of duty you'd ideally want. Just know that we are not politicians and have no pretensions of considering ourselves VIPs, so please, while here, be part of the family. Come in when you need anything and let us know how we can help. I hope this duty isn't any longer than it needs to be.'

Gaikwad straightened as he responded, looking me in the eyes. 'Major saab, we've been briefed. We know exactly who you are. You served with the 9th Paras, won an Ashoka Chakra, killed a terrorist in unarmed combat in Mumbai. The newspapers were shy about what happened in Afghanistan, but we heard rumours of the sort that sound like they might just be true. It is an honour to protect your family.'

I nodded and went inside. An email was waiting for me. The Group CEO of Bharat Gas had accepted my application to go on a six-month sabbatical to 'sort out family issues'. The cover stories were in place with a speed that stunned me—the IB had produced some fake chatter about jihadis targeting my family. The resultant extra protection would make sure Zoya and Aman were as safe as they could be, and I had some time off to supposedly spend with them.

Phadke had come over for breakfast and as he saw the hard-looking NSG men, he patted me on my shoulder. 'It must be more serious than we thought. I just got an email that spooks were coming to comb for any electronic bugs, and that you had suddenly got the kind of security cover only fat, corrupt politicians get. Now I hear you're off to Delhi on some fancy government jet. I hope you're not getting yourself into a deeper soup?'

In reality, I was jumping off the deep end once again. There was another letter in my hand, printed on stationery that indicated it came from the prime minister's office. It had been hand-delivered a couple of hours earlier, calling me for a meeting in Delhi the next morning.

'Trouble? Not at all. Just routine briefing I suppose that will be a waste of everybody's time.'

Phadke looked me straight in the eye. I knew he didn't buy a word of what I was saying.

'Aadi, I've spent my whole life being a cop. I know when someone is lying. You may be a very good soldier, but you are a poor liar. Take care and know that if you need anything from me, I'll be there. This time, you don't even need a bottle of single malt to get me to co-operate.'

He smiled as he left, but I had seen the hard glint in his eyes.

I felt Zoya's hand on my shoulder. 'Worried?'

'Yes. About you, Aman. It would have been different if it had just been me…'

She grabbed me from behind, holding me tight, and I turned around as she buried her head in my chest. 'Aadi, remember what you told me when we were both in danger the last time? You told me you couldn't sit by while others were in danger. I want having me and Aman in your life to make you stronger, not weaker. Go be the man you are, the man I fell in love with. We know someone like you is out there and needs help, and he needs to come back to those waiting for him at home. I can't be so selfish as to ask you to stay here and ignore him.'

I must have cashed in on all my good deeds in life to have had someone like Zoya marry me, and as I told her as much, she laughed. 'Just come back to me.'

'I promise.'

***

Phadke had commented about me setting out on a luxurious jet, but the less glamorous reality was that I was sitting crammed between equipment and soldiers on a C-130 Spectre transport plane headed to the Hindon Air Force Base near Delhi. The soldiers kept to themselves, though a few nodded at me. They all wore the maroon berets of the Special Forces, as I once had, and if any of them wondered what a man in civilian clothes was doing there, they said nothing. I knew the feeling. We would often have people ride with us, and we assumed they were politicians along for a thrill, babus out to finally see what the real world was, or, more often than not, spooks. Since I doubt I looked like a politician or bureaucrat, the soldiers must have assumed I was a spook. But they gave me the space I needed to get ready for the upcoming meeting.

We were met at the airbase by a government car that whisked me away to South Block. I was led into a large, wood-panelled room and sat on one of the chairs around a long conference table. I poured myself a glass of water as I waited, wondering what was in store. The door swung open and in walked a man whose face I had often seen in the news and whom I had spoken to several times when in the Korengal Valley. Ajay Gopal, the National Security Advisor to the PM. He had been the head of the Intelligence Bureau under the old government and that he continued to thrive under the new regime spoke of his competence. I had never met him before, but my old CO had never had a bad thing to say about him, which was high praise for a combat soldier talking about a bureaucrat.

'Keep sitting, Major. An old friend briefed me about you and your circumstances. Truth be told, he saved my life twice during operations, so when he says I should pay attention to something, I don't second-guess him. After Afghanistan, I had asked if you wanted to work for us, and you said no. I don't like being rejected, but when my old mentor told me you changed your mind, I had to listen.'

I sent up a silent thanks to Dhar for once again coming through.

'Now, I'd like to hear it all, and I'd like to see this paper.'

When I finished my story and handed him the paper, the door opened and someone else walked in. I froze when I saw that it was the prime minister himself. The letter I had received had come from his office, but I had assumed I'd meet with some senior officers. It had never struck me that the PM himself would meet me. He smiled and sat down on a chair across the table from me and nodded at me to hand him the paper.

There was the word 'Invictus' and under it the symbol I had tattooed on my upper back. A winged dagger, with the Hindi word Balidaan under it. A symbol that I and my brothers in arms had sworn by and one our enemies had learned to fear. The symbol of the Indian Army's Para Special Forces.

I didn't know what 'Invictus' had to do with it all, but I knew what the symbol meant, and it convinced me I had done the right thing coming to Delhi.

One of my brothers was in Chinese custody.

I came back the next day for a meeting at six in the evening. This time, Gopal and the prime minister were joined by General Subir Singh, the Chief of Army Staff.

'If they have our boy, we will get him back.' I could see the veins standing up, almost to the point of popping, in General Singh's neck. He looked straight at me. 'Major, what do you think?'

'Why don't we just confront the Chinese with this? Clearly they were willing to kill innocent people on our soil to stop this paper coming to light.'

Gopal shook his head. 'Major, as of now, they have no idea that the paper is in your hands or that we have seen it. For all they know, the secret ended with Anita. If we confront them, they will just deny everything. They could just say this is a forgery we're using to put pressure on them with our current border tensions. Even worse, if this prisoner is still alive, they could just make him disappear.'

I clenched my fists in frustration, not knowing how to express what I felt in front of such senior leaders.

The prime minister smiled at me. 'Major, what's on your mind?'

'Sir, if I may speak, this man seems to have been a Para. I don't know how he ended up in Chinese hands, but can we abandon him? Don't we owe it to him to not forget his sacrifice?'

The PM looked at Gopal, as if asking a question, and Gopal nodded, as I continued. 'I just can't figure out why he would write the word "Invictus". He clearly cut himself to write this message in his own blood. What does the Chinese writing on the other side mean?'

Gopal looked at me with narrowed eyes. 'Major, you have done your bit. You have brought to us information that clearly is of importance to us, and we will act on it. But you need to decide whether you are just a concerned citizen or something more. If it's the former, then you need to leave since any further discussion is highly confidential.'

The sudden shift in tone caught me off guard, but I knew what Gopal was asking. Are you in all the way or not?

He silently handed me a piece of paper. I scanned the contents. I would be subject to the Official Secrets Act; I could face prosecution for revealing details of what I saw or heard; for a six-month period, I would put myself in the employ of the government as a contractor and could not work for anyone else. In short, I was signing myself away to the government. To be fair, it wasn't as if they expected me to do all this out of a feeling of patriotism. My eyes widened when I saw that a sum of rupees 3 lakhs would be deposited in my account every month and that if I died, my family would get a compensation of rupees 2 crore.

There was all the legal fine print that meant you held very few cards but as I looked at the paper on the table, I realized I wouldn't be doing this just for the money. I would do this for Anita, Randhawa, and above all, for that soldier in captivity, wondering if the country he had killed and been ready to die for ever really gave a damn.

I did give a damn. I picked up the pen and signed. 'Tell me what I need to do, sir.'

'This is footage from a drone over Ladakh. What do you see, Major?'

It took me a mere few seconds to respond to General Singh. 'Sir, those are muzzle flashes from rifles. And I saw several mortar rounds explode. The media talks of scuffles and occasional fights, but this looks like war!'

The PM tapped his fingers on the table. 'The media doesn't know how close we are to all-out war. I've spoken to the Chinese, and they of course lay the blame on some rogue commander, but this is orchestrated by them—to test how we respond. Do you see what would happen if the paper became public? The media would go crazy, public opinion would demand we react in a strong way, and we would indeed have an all-out war on our hands.'

'With all due respect, sir, we cannot just ignore the paper or not try to find our man.'

Gopal took over. 'Major, you've operated against the Pakistanis and to some extent they're like us. They hit us, we hit them, and so it goes. What you see is what you get. With the Chinese, it's different. More than actual action on the ground and its outcome, it's saving face that matters. If we push too hard, their leadership will lose face and they will push back, hard.'

Call me a dumb soldier, but I didn't see what was wrong with that. 'Sir, if they push, we push back. After all, we'd be doing it for all the right reasons.'

The prime minister smiled. 'Major, the man who wrote this paper is indeed a lot like you—a Para who joined RAW. He was on a highly classified mission, for which he was codenamed Invictus. He has been missing for over a year, and now we know where he is. Thanks to using his own blood, we have a positive DNA match.'

He got up and began pacing up and down. 'You are a veteran too, Major. Your motto is "Balidaan". And I assure you, the sacrifices made by the soldier who wrote this paper will not be forgotten. But if we make this public, we react to what the Chinese do. We lose the initiative. The Chinese writing on the other side is in some sort of code, which we have not cracked yet. Till we do that, we don't know what leverage we have, and why they are so desperate to get this paper back. My guess is the Chinese text is what is making them jumpy. We will act, but at a time and in circumstances of our choosing, when we have the advantage.'

I saw the prime minister in a whole new light. He was known to be a great orator, a disciplinarian, a visionary, but now I saw a streak to him that made him a leader to follow, and an opponent to fear.

———— ✦ ————

For the next week, our life limped back to some semblance of normalcy. Gopal was clear that whoever was watching me would have to believe I was continuing with life as usual. We got Aman back into preschool, though I dropped him off and picked him up every day, and having two NSG commandos standing guard outside a preschool was anything but normal. Zoya's company was a bit more understanding when her boss got a call from Delhi. She was given a part-time working arrangement where she could take care of most of her duties from home, or, in our case, a heavily guarded guest house.

'Really, Aadi, did the PMO have to call him? Isn't that borderline intimidation?' She said it with a smile, but I could see the hint of criticism in her eyes. She didn't want any special favours because of what I had signed up for.

'Zo, I would love to say that we can and get back to our lives as they were, but that's impossible. If I have to go through with this, I can't do it if I'm hurting you or your career. I just asked if someone from the government could explain to your company the unique circumstances we are in. I had no idea the PMO would call.'

She smiled, the tension dissipating, and she held me close. 'What's most important to me is that you are safe, and, yes, that you see this through.'

When I had served in the army, I had not been married and had never been able to relate to what some of the married officers said about their wives also serving with them. Now I knew what they meant.

The satellite phone Gopal had given me rang just then. He had been clear that all communication with the government was to be through this secure satellite line and both Zoya and I had been given new encrypted phones with instructions to limit those we shared the numbers with.

'Major, buckle up. We have a plan. As the PM said, we need to get the initiative back.'

'Great, sir. I'm happy we're taking the initiative.'

'Indeed, Major. We have a plan to get this assassin to reveal himself. Once we get him, we can know more about who's driving this—whether it's an official Chinese government project or led by non-state actors—and also learn what's on the paper, since our geeks haven't cracked the code yet. It'll help take one of their pieces off the board and give us more leverage by helping us know where they are holding our man.'

'How do we get him to reveal himself?'

'Why, Major, we dangle him an irresistible bait.'

I had a bad feeling where this was going. He didn't need to say it—I knew I was going to be that bait.

As plans went, it wasn't a bad one. Perhaps a bit too clever for its own good, but that is true of most plans cooked up in conference rooms, whether you were talking about the corporate world or the world I was operating in. There is bluff, double bluff, and so much smoke and mirrors that I was convinced of two things. First, that the smartest geeks didn't work in high-paying consulting jobs but in some back office deep in South Block; and second, that these men hadn't actually ever had to face the prospect of being killed if their plans went wrong. If our plan went belly up, I resolved I would pay these fellows a visit and beat them to a pulp with the thick stacks of PowerPoint slides they seemed to revel in generating.

Either way, there I was at the lobby of the Taj Mahal Palace hotel. The geeks had thought this part through well, I would grant them. They had put out fake chatter that some jihadis were planning a repeat of the 26/11 attacks on the anniversary of the event. That gave them perfect cover to have heavy-duty police presence in South Mumbai and a squad of commandos hovering nearby. Traffic was a mess, and if all those Mumbaikars knew I was to blame for screwing up their Sunday, I was sure there would be even more people after my blood.

As it was, that list wasn't short. I had no idea how the geeks knew to get the word out, but the media was all over the story. So there was a real risk that some jihadi wannabe could drop by, but Gopal sounded pretty confident that they had most known terror cells under watch. Of course, the security presence would probably make a bit of a dent in the revenues of the restaurants at the Taj, but what everyone was counting on was that our Chinese friends would take the separate bait that had been dangled for them.

By now, Gopal's analysts were sure the Chinese knew more about me than my family did, given their own analysts were supposed to be pretty good at prying into people's lives. So they knew my service record, my role in Mumbai, and would want to get back at me for the pain I had caused their boys in Afghanistan. I suspected Gopal was betting on that, if the assassin was indeed the man I had encountered in Afghanistan.

As I sat in the lobby, I wondered where all this chatter was observed and read. I chuckled as I imagined spies and terrorists of all hues bumping into each other on dark web message boards and forums. Did they have handles they could recognize each other by? Did they form friendships? Did any of them ever meet there and fall in love and then discover they were tasked to kill each other? I'd let Bollywood develop that line of thinking further. For now, I had more immediate concerns.

My mobile rang. The peon from the office.

'Sir, where are you?'

'In the lobby. Come in.'

'Are you sure, sir? I've never been inside such a fancy place before.'

'Of course I'm sure. Come in. Do you have the envelope?'

'Yes, sir. It's with me.'

I sat back, every instinct on alert. The peon had called my mobile a day ago, informing me that Anita had left an envelope for me and that he had just discovered it while cleaning up my cubicle. Gopal had told me the best lies were those that had a foundation in truth, so the peon was puzzled at being asked to make the call, but he sounded convincing enough because indeed, Anita had left a package for me. The real peon had now disappeared, being told to take a special paid holiday for a month.

Gopal had insisted he call my mobile number on the assumption that it was being tapped. Whether that assumption was true, we would find out very soon.

The man on his way to meet me was one of Gopal's men. As the revolving door swung, a thin man walked in wearing a bright shirt and slightly tattered jeans, looking nervously around him, much as an office peon might when he entered the lobby of a luxury hotel for the first time. I knew spies were good liars, now I saw they were pretty good actors as well. As the man walked towards me, I reminded myself that while I had little option but to trust Gopal, I wouldn't make it a habit. The last time I had trusted a spy hadn't ended all that well. I had been captured by terrorists, waterboarded and nearly beheaded on camera.

The man handed me an envelope. 'Here it is.'

As he moved to leave, I stood and looked around me. Where would a Chinese assassin come for me? Not in a crowded hotel lobby, that much was obvious. Gopal's men had come up with an analysis that the best place to lure them would be the alleyways behind the Taj.

I called Zoya on my mobile, as had been planned. 'Hey, Zo. Am near the Taj. Remember the bag you liked in that shop behind the Taj? Should I pick it up?'

'Thanks, sweetheart. Take care.'

As I hung up, I could hear the tension in her words and hoped the Chinese wouldn't pick it up, or, being so close to the paper, wouldn't care. There was a police constable waiting outside, the guard assigned by Phadke. I called him next.

'Talpade, I'm stepping out to buy something. I'll meet you in front of the Taj in five minutes.'

Poor Talpade, who knew nothing of the plan, sputtered in anxiety. 'Phadke Sir told me to not let you out of my sight.'

'Have you seen the security today? There must be a bloody battalion of soldiers and commandos around Nariman Point.'

I stepped out through a side exit and circled back, passing the Starbucks behind the Taj and heading towards one of the small alleys. It was six in the evening and, in what passed for winter in Mumbai, it was already a bit chilly and dark.

I could hear Gopal himself in my earpiece. The fact that he was so personally involved told me just how seriously the government was taking this and gave me a bit of confidence that I wasn't just going to be left bleeding to death in an alleyway. 'Keep going. We have eyes on you.'

'They must be well hidden.'

He chuckled. 'They are, and the drone above you is too high to see.'

Shit. I looked up involuntarily. They had a drone monitoring this. I wondered just what kind of power game between India and China I had got myself caught up in. Then I thought of the soldier who had written on the paper and reminded myself that it was still worth it to stick my neck out into harm's way.

'Hello! Fancy seeing you here, and that too without your uniformed babysitters.'

I froze as Ravi walked towards me, a broad grin on his face. Gopal's best-laid plans had just gone for a toss.

'You don't even have time to have a proper conversation nowadays? What are you mixed up in?'

'Ravi, what are you doing here?'

He took a step toward me. 'It's a free country, last time I checked. I had lunch with a friend, did some shopping and was picking up some kebabs for dinner before I headed back home. Detailed enough for you?'

I could hear Gopal whispering in my ear. 'Get him out of there!'

I started to walk past Ravi. 'I'm in a hurry. I'll call you later.'

As I tried to walk past him, he grabbed my arm, his grip not much weaker than it had been when he had been my trainer all those years ago. 'I've known you since the time you were a kid who signed up dreaming of being a commando. Something's wrong. Do you need help?'

I gently took his hand off my arm and leaned towards him. 'Ravi, please let me pass and get out of this alley.'

Just then, there was a blur of motion towards my right. I moved to the left out of pure instinct, a motion that saved my life as the blade aimed at my midsection passed within inches of me. I turned to see two men, a lean, tall, masked man and a shorter but heavyset man with his face up to his eyes covered by a scarf. Both carried long, thin knives.

The dance had begun. But where the hell were the commandos that Gopal had promised?

'Send them in…'

I barely got time to complete my shout as the masked man moved in for another strike. He knew what he was doing. Fluid footwork, economy of movement and good balance. I would have admired him longer if I had not been preoccupied with trying to stay alive. I moved back, blocking his blow with my left hand, wincing as he drew blood. That was what I hated about knife fights and what most movies conveniently ignored. If you found yourself in one, chances were you'd get cut. He saw the envelope in my right hand, and he whistled as the second man moved in.

Where the hell were the commandos?

Just then, I heard gunfire behind us. Shit, were there other attackers engaging the soldiers meant to be my rescuers? In that case, I was on my own.

The shorter man moved in, not nearly as graceful, but when you outnumber your enemy two to one and you have knives while your adversary has a piece of paper to defend himself with, form doesn't really matter much to the final outcome.

That was when Ravi moved in. I had forgotten he was there. The two attackers had clearly not paid attention to someone they didn't perceive as a threat—an old man, carrying a shopping bag. But he was no ordinary old man, but a former officer in the Paras. One who was long retired, slower, less fit than he had once been, but what he remembered and what he could bring to bear was still devastating. His right hand snaked out and struck the man on the nape of the neck and the man stumbled towards me. I saw his pupils dilate as he passed out, my old trainer's blow no less accurate than it had been a decade ago. What he had begun, I finished as I struck the man at the base of his nose with my outstretched palm with predictable and deadly results. Bones shattered, pushed to the back of the nose into the brain. Instant death.

The masked assassin wasted no time, nor was he fazed that he was now outnumbered. He spun on his heel and stabbed Ravi. A hand snaking out with a speed I had rarely seen. Perhaps in his prime, Ravi might have blocked it, but now in this struggle between speed and experience, speed won. The assassin stabbed Ravi and pulled his blade out in one fluid motion. As Ravi crumpled to the ground, I roared in fury and charged.

Never fight angry. That had been drummed into us by our trainers. Be pissed off, be driven by the desire to kill the bastard in front of you, but never give into blind rage. Good advice that had served me well, but seeing the man who had been like a father to me bleeding in front of me, I forgot that advice.

The envelope that the Chinese coveted so much was the first to go. I flung the envelope, Frisbee style, at him. He had come for it and he couldn't resist looking at it as it fell to the ground. That gave me a window of opportunity to move in closer and land two quick blows to his midsection. They would have cracked the ribs on a lesser man, but as it was, they must have done some damage as he staggered back, giving me time to pull out my Swiss Army knife.

I got a good look at his eyes, and I quickly realized two things. First that he was actually smiling, by the way his eyes contracted, and the twinkle in them. Second, that that the eyes seemed familiar. This was the same man I had met in the Korengal Valley and then again, when masquerading as a pirate in the South China Sea.

He came in fast, swinging, feinting, stabbing. Well, it took two to tango and if he wanted to dance, I was happy to oblige. His right hand shot out and in mid-strike, he threw the knife to his left hand, which he brought towards my neck in a deadly arc. Very nifty, and nearly worked, except I blocked his blow with my right hand and caught him on the cheek with my left elbow. As he staggered back, he cut me on the right shoulder and we both took a step back. He was good and he had a longer knife.

My Swiss Army knife was fine for scaring suburban detectives, but against this guy, it was like bringing a letter-opener to a knife fight. He came in again, knife seeking my stomach. I wasn't going to stand around waiting to be disembowelled, so his knife met thin air as I pivoted out of the way, grabbed his wrist, and used his momentum to throw him to the ground. As he fell, I sent up a silent thanks to an old Israeli buddy who had trained us in Krav Maga. Of course, that didn't do much to improve my Chinese buddy's mood. He said a string of things in Chinese I assumed would not have passed the censor board's approval and started to move in for another attack, when I heard Gopal in my ear.

'The commandos are on the way. Hold him there!' Easy for him to say, sitting wherever he was.

As the man slashed down, I blocked with my left hand and brought my own right hand up towards his neck. I wasn't surprised to find that he blocked my blow, given the levels of training he had already demonstrated. There we stood, locked in a struggle where neither of us really seemed to be able to force the issue. But that was okay with me. Success for him was killing me and getting away. Success for me was holding him long enough for the commandos to grab him.

I heard Gopal screaming in my ear, and I wished he would just shut up.

We were locked together, our faces inches from each other, every muscle in our body straining. He tried to knee me in the groin, but I brought my left leg up and across to block him and slowly but surely began to wear down his left hand, bringing the blade in my right hand closer to him.

His eyes narrowed as Gopal screamed again, and at such close quarters, he either heard him or just saw the earpiece and knew it was a trap. He moved his head back slightly, and even as I realized what was coming, I also knew I was too late in reacting. He brought his head forward, butting me in the face. I managed to twist my face to the right, saving my nose from being broken, but the searing pain of the blow made me lose my grip enough for him to twist loose and disengage.

I could hear the commandos shouting behind me now and the masked assassin looked straight into my eyes, as if wondering whether he had time to try to finish me. He knelt, grabbed the envelope and ran off into the alley behind him.

Four commandos rushed past me, but unless they got lucky, I doubted very much that they would get him. He was a professional, and I was sure he had a getaway planned.

I rushed to Ravi, cradling his limp body, screaming for an ambulance as the man I had considered to be no less than my father lay bleeding in my arms.

'You better have a bloody good reason for what you did there.'

I was sitting outside the ICU of the hospital while Phadke ranted at me. He had every right. He had been in charge of providing me protection, and I had walked away from the guard he had assigned. He had no idea I was obeying other masters, and I wasn't sure I could tell him about them. Rekha and Zoya were next to me, Aman sitting quietly by them in his stroller.

I got up as the doctor came out. He didn't even wait for me to ask the question. 'He's stable, doing as well as one might expect. No major internal damage. He was very healthy, so that helped. But he's lost a lot of blood, so we'll keep him under observation for a few days.'

As the doctor walked off, I took Phadke aside. 'I'm sorry things turned out the way they did, but I wouldn't have put myself or Ravi into harm's way unless I had a good reason.'

He looked at me, his shrewd eyes showing that his mind was doing all kinds of calculations. 'Given the mess you have been involved in, would it be correct to assume these reasons have something to do with New Delhi and above my pay grade?'

When he saw me hesitate, he backed off, though it was clear he was still very pissed off. 'Aadi, I don't mean to pry, and you can tell me that I have no need to know. But can a friend give you some free advice?'

'Sure...'

He leaned towards me, speaking in a whisper. 'Never trust a spy. I thought you would have figured that out given what happened the last time you got mixed up with that lot.'

With that, he walked off, whistling a tune as Zoya came up to me. 'Phadke seems happy enough.'

'He should be. He's got a real job and a career, no assassins out to kill him, and his loved ones aren't in danger of being killed just because they know him.'

I realized just how bitter I sounded the moment the words came out, and I was about to say something to soften the blow when Zoya took my hand and leaned against my chest.

'Aadi, none of us asked for this. I know you tried to avoid getting involved, but these bastards have threatened our family and almost killed Ravi, and I want them to pay. So don't regret the choices you have made, but think about how you can see them through.'

I held her, and anyone seeing us from a distance might think that she was leaning on me for strength. I knew only too well at that moment I was deriving courage from her.

A week later, I was back in Delhi. Gopal was at his desk with three men I had never seen before. He never introduced us, and I didn't ask. Gopal was in a foul mood, and when he began ranting, I thought it prudent to not add my own frustration to it.

'Lucky bastard. Two stupid kids set off firecrackers near our patrol. With all the news about the terror threat we had spread, a couple of commandos thought they were under attack and began firing. Luckily none of those kids was hit and melted away into the slums. We found firecrackers. If only the commandos had got there in time, we would have had him.'

'You had a drone overhead. How did he get away?'

Gopal looked up. 'He had that planned. Drone and CCTV footage shows him running into the kitchen of a restaurant from the back. We never saw him afterwards. He may well have changed and melted away among the customers and staff. Now, are you sure the man you fought is the one you say he was? I've had these analysts burning the midnight oil to isolate who he could be. They told me they made some progress yesterday and that's why you are here.'

I thought back to those eyes and nodded. I was as sure as I was ever going to be.

One of the analysts opened up a laptop and tapped a few keys. It was the same blurry footage of the confrontation between Indian and Chinese soldiers I had seen on TV. He pressed some more keys and the image sharpened. As he zoomed in, I saw myself looking into the same eyes. The eyes of the man who had nearly killed Ravi. The same man whom I had met on a remote island near Vietnam and on a remote hilltop in Afghanistan.

'That's him.'

As the analyst froze the image, he brought up a screen that showed the man, perhaps a few years younger, wearing a uniform.

The analyst looked up at me. 'Captain Zhang Shi Hu.

Chinese Special Forces. Member of an elite unit called Oriental Sword that was part of the Beijing Military Region. Tough bastards, but I suspect you know their sort.'

I thought back to the fight in the alley. Yes, I knew the sort all right.

The analyst continued. 'No real trace of him for the last few years. He's been showing up in all kinds of places, so our hypothesis is that he is employed by the MSS.'

'MSS?'

Gopal answered that one. 'Ministry of State Security. They are, I guess, our counterparts, combining the Intelligence Bureau and RAW's mandates in one organization. Do a lot of nasty business overseas. Making Hong Kong publishers disappear, going after dissidents, and so on. Someone of the captain's talents would have been a real asset to them. What you learned in Afghanistan connects the dots. We were never sure what Unit 7 really was. Now it seems it is a deep black unit run by the MSS. I suppose drugs and piracy help them fund their ops and get their men into all sorts of places where they have an agenda. It's our good fortune that you bumped into him in Afghanistan, so we now know who he is.'

'Sir, what do your analysts think will happen now that they have the fake paper?'

'As for you, Aaditya, things could go one of two ways. First, the Chinese by now know the paper they have wasn't what they were looking for. Just a bunch of sheets from a corporate meeting, so they may assume you know nothing and leave you alone. In that case, you might be able to get back to your life as it was. On the other hand, they may think you're deeply involved and part of setting up the ambush. In that case, they may come for you again.'

It wasn't me that I was so worried about, but I didn't want to live with the chance that someone, perhaps Zhang or someone like him, would come for Zoya or Aman.

Gopal was studying me with a curious expression. 'Our code breakers have been on the job, and cracked only two words. "Lotus" and "Camel". There are two other words, but when we tried decoding them, we got two words that seem to mean nothing—"redirection" and "blowback".'

I sat up straight. Lotus was the code name for the drug-smuggling ring whose home base I had helped wreck in Afghanistan.

'If nothing else, this helps us link the Chinese, or at least this Unit 7, directly to the Mumbai attacks and the incident in Afghanistan. That's embarrassing enough for them and gives us a lot of leverage. Camel may well be another op of theirs, but till we crack the rest we don't know.'

Gopal dismissed the analysts.

'We can of course take proactive action and ensure we get to the bottom of this paper mystery, get our man back and take Zhang off the board. We may not be the only ones looking for him or his Unit 7 buddies.'

That got my attention as Gopal continued. 'Once we heard from you that you'd met this man with the pirates, we activated our assets in South East Asia, and guess what? As they scoured through their contacts in all sorts of unsavoury quarters, from drug smugglers to arms dealers to Chinese triads, they realized someone else had been following Zhang's trail. Not coming at him from the angle we have, but from contacts gathered from Ross and his buddies. We worked our way back, almost like following a trail of crumbs. The more we worked our way back, the more we realized that whoever this person was, he was not just fishing for information. At various stages, the links to Zhang and Unit 7 that he found ended up dead. Usually with a single bullet to the head fired from a sniper rifle from long range.'

It took me a while to process what he was saying, and then he spelled it out.

'Aman Karzai. Major, your friend has been busy. We've tallied at least ten killings in the last year—all of them men tied to Ross or his pals, all of them linked to the drug ring you uncovered in Afghanistan. Of late, he seems to be getting closer to the Chinese. Two months ago, a Chinese general was shot on vacation in Egypt by a sniper. Before that, a couple of Pakistani generals in the UAE, who we know were on the Chinese payroll. The media said these were terror attacks. But no jihadi groups were involved. If Unit 7 or their Chinese bosses were behind Lotus, they were directly responsible for the death of his mother and much of his family. For him, this is a blood debt, and he will keep going.'

'How does that impact our plans?'

Gopal leaned over to me with a twinkle in his eyes, and I remembered Phadke's advice to never trust a spy.

'We've sacrificed two good assets to get intelligence that puts Zhang in Vietnam right now. We've leaked some of that through double agents and contacts to get Karzai's attention. I have no doubt he will come for him. We can't launch an op in Vietnam, but with Karzai in play, it both helps and complicates things.'

I could never understand how spies thought, but usually their plans were too clever for their own good. As Gopal continued, I realized it was not just clever, it was utterly ruthless.

'Tempting as it is to have Karzai put a bullet in Zhang's head, if he does so we lose our opportunity to find out where our man is being held. But there's no way we can go in all guns blazing into the middle of Ho Chi Minh City. The diplomatic consequences would be disastrous, and the Chinese probably have more assets on the ground. So, we're proposing to use Karzai's services without him knowing it and put you in the mix, working with him to try to get Zhang alive. We will have a small, discreet snatch team in place to grab him. That we can manage without creating too much of a ruckus with the Vietnamese.'

I really didn't like where this was going.

'Major, remember you signed up for this. I could order you, but out of respect for your services, I can allow you to back out, but there's no guarantee Zhang won't come for you again.'

As I looked at Gopal, I had to try hard to contain my fury. Unlike what you see in the movies, there are often no clear-cut good or bad guys. In his own way, Gopal was as ruthless as Zhang or his masters, happy to sacrifice pawns like me or Karzai to achieve his objectives. The only thing that kept me from walking out was that Gopal had a point—I could never be sure my family was safe if Zhang was out there. That and the fact that somewhere out there was a man like me, kept prisoner in a cell, thinking that his country had forgotten him.

'What do I need to do?'

'Here they come!' The captain of the small cargo ship shouted out the words two more times as the speedboat approached his ship. He almost laughed as he contemplated trying to make a run for it. There was no way he could and from what he had heard from comrades, running or fighting only made things worse. Maybe the pirates would take money and food and leave them alone. The cargo that he was carrying, consisting largely of imported cosmetics headed for the grey market in Vietnam, would perhaps not interest the pirates. But who knew? If some boxes of counterfeit perfumes or creams got them to go away, it was a small price to pay.

His son came up, knuckles white on the railing, as the captain looked at the approaching boat through his binoculars. 'Tran, I see four men, all carrying assault rifles.'

'Father, we have twelve men on board, and at least eight of us are young and fit. We can gather up iron rods and axes and when the bastards get on board, we can take them down.'

The captain smiled, both proud of his son's courage and touched by his naïveté. 'My son, one man with a Kalashnikov could take down half of us if he opened up on full auto. Three or four of them would massacre us.'

Tran was quiet, but that didn't mean he was satisfied with his father's answer.

The captain called the rest of his crew up. 'Listen, all of you. We all know friends who've been hit, and we've been lucky in the last four years that we haven't attracted pirates. Today, luck ran out.'

A burly man, the captain's cousin, grumbled. 'Tran's right. We can take them. We work so hard to earn some money, and these goons think they can just take it away.'

The captain touched his cousin lightly on the shoulder. 'I know how you feel, and I know for all of us this is not just business, this is our life. So it guts me. When these bastards come here, it's as if they've invaded my home.'

That got angry grunts all around, and the captain held out his hands to cool his comrades down. 'But I was in the army and I know what these guys can do. Most of them are trained, they're armed, and they are ruthless. I don't want to risk losing you guys. We can earn the money again, as long as we stay alive.'

He could see that his comrades were not happy, but he didn't need them to be happy, as long as they all stayed alive. He took one more look through his binoculars. 'They're maybe one kilometre out. Don't resist and don't do anything stupid.'

The men nodded, and then the captain heard another

voice, this time in English. 'Captain, perhaps I could be of assistance.'

Every one of the gathered men turned to look at the speaker. Many of the men spoke only rudimentary English, but over the last seven days, they had come to accept the passenger they had on board. They might not have had a lot to talk about with him, but he was quiet, polite, and happy to help out on whatever chore he was given. He certainly didn't try to lord it over with the airs of someone who had paid so much money to be on board.

The captain didn't know who he was, but a close friend whom he had once served with had vouched for him. The $3,000 the stranger had paid in cash certainly had not hurt. The captain winced as he realized the pirates would likely take that money as well.

The passenger walked up and looked over the captain's shoulder. 'Expecting company?'

The captain handed him the binoculars and repeated what he had told his comrades in English about who was on the approaching and what lay ahead. The man took another look at the fast-approaching pirate ship and then took the captain aside. 'I can take them out for you, if you swear to not tell anyone what I did.'

The captain's blank expression said it all. He had no idea what the man was talking about. The man reached out and shook the captain's shoulder. 'Look, if they get on board and search me, they'll find things that will get me and you in trouble. We don't have time. Ask all your men to go inside and lock the door. It's better if they don't see what happens.'

The captain just looked on, as the man then proceeded to take charge.

'Go inside. I will lock the door from the outside. I will negotiate with them. I have money and will offer it to them if they leave this ship alone. Also, stop the engines. We cannot run and there's no point in making it any harder than it needs to be.'

The men had all heard of the sum the man had paid to be on board, and nodded. As the men rushed inside, the captain walked up to the man. 'Why did you ask them to stop the engines?'

The man smiled and the captain felt a chill go through him. The smile was not one of humour, but that of a predator who has scented prey. The captain had been in the Vietnamese army and had seen some men like that, men in special forces.

The man handed the binoculars back to the captain. 'You were in the army, right? Use the binoculars. Help me.'

The captain gulped as he wondered what was coming. 'How?'

The man reached for the guitar case he carried with him. 'I need a spotter.'

--◆--

When the first pirate lurched back and fell off the boat, his three companions were stunned. They called out to him and threw a life vest towards him. They assumed he had stumbled and fallen. There was no reason to imagine that their friend had just been shot through by a bullet fired from over six hundred metres away from the small ship that they had been approaching. The pirate leader killed the engine and took a closer look at the man's body floating in the water, a barely discernible pool of red spreading around his body. He looked back at the ship ahead of them and raised his binoculars to his eyes. His brain was still processing what he was seeing, when a bullet smashed through the right lens of the binoculars and passed through his eye and brain, exiting out the back. When he fell, there was no doubt among his two remaining mates what had happened. One of them raised his AK-47 and began firing.

The captain flinched as the bullets raked the water in front of his ship. The pirate had opened up on full auto, in shock at the death of his leader, and had hardly thought straight enough to aim or to realize that he needed to compensate for the swell and rise of the sea and the extreme range at which he was firing. The captain processed that because he had served as an infantryman for a decade, but even he had flinched. It was hard not to when bullets were coming at you.

Not so the man next to him, who was peering through the scope of his rifle. His voice was calm and even, with no hint of emotion. 'Captain, tell me when the idiot pauses to reload.'

A second later the captain spoke up. 'Now.'

A soft puff, and a single 7.62mm bullet left the barrel of the Dragunov, passing through the suppressor and flying unerringly towards the pirate, who had raised his rifle to his shoulder again. The bullet took him in the neck and he went down. That left just one pirate, standing there staring in horror at the bodies of his comrades. He raised his hands, hoping whoever had killed his mates would spare him.

The captain saw the sniper's mouth moving rapidly as he stared through the scope. 'What are you doing?'

The sniper replied without taking his eye off the scope. 'I'm praying to Allah for forgiveness. I don't want to kill an unarmed man, but I cannot risk him telling anyone about his friends being killed here. I wish they had not come upon us. I wish I did not have to kill them.'

Then he pulled the trigger.

***

Tran walked into the small room their passenger had been allotted. The man was kneeling on a mat, praying with his hands held up in front of him. Tran waited for him to finish, and he looked up at Tran, smiling.

'Is there anything I can do to help? Your father said we would make landfall soon.'

Tran sat down next to the man. He had gone to college and planned to start work in a shipping company soon. He would have loved to continue doing these runs with his father, but the man had been insistent that he needed to create a better future for himself. As a result of his education, he was much better at English than any of the other crew, so he was also the most comfortable at conversing with their passenger.

'No, not much to help with now. What happened with those pirates?'

The man looked up at Tran, his eyes boring into the young man's. Tran had always seen their passenger as a quiet, friendly man who kept to himself. Looking into his eyes now, he wondered if he should have asked the question. Then the smile was back.

'I don't know. They seem to have had a disagreement and fought among themselves.'

Tran nodded and began to get up and the man waved for him to wait. As the man got up, he reached into his bag and took out an envelope and handed it to Tran.

'What's this?'

The man smiled. 'Your father told me you're well-educated and wants you to make a fresh start. He has worked really hard to provide for you and your family, and, like all good fathers, wants you to have a safer, more stable life. This is something to get you started. Don't tell him I gave you this. He's a proud man but take this as a gift from someone who knows how important it is to get a helping hand sometimes to take your life on the right path.'

Tran walked back to his small cot and whistled as he peeled open the envelope to find two thousand dollars in cash.

The captain called out to all his men on the deck. 'Landfall in less than an hour. Lights out and keep it quiet. We don't want to attract any unnecessary attention this close.'

The men cheered and then all the lights went off as the ship proceeded quietly in the dark. The captain sensed someone behind him and heard their passenger at his shoulder.

'We're almost there. I don't know who you are, but thank you.'

'Captain, thank you for getting me here. Just keep what you saw quiet. I have many enemies who would take extreme measures to get to me, and you would be putting yourself and your family at risk by alerting anyone to my presence here.'

The captain nodded, wondering what had brought this stranger on this journey. He knew there was no point in asking, but he did ask anyway. 'Why are you coming to Vietnam?'

The man smiled in the darkness. 'I have some debts to repay.'

'Dada. Dada.'

I held Aman up as we sat with his toys scattered around us. He had barely begun to string together words, but the worry he couldn't yet put into words showed in his big eyes. His little life had been turned upside down. He didn't know what the guards outside our home and his school meant, but he sensed that his daddy was going away and his mommy didn't seem happy about it.

'Dude, I'll be back real soon. I just need to do some job at work.'

'Job?'

A great question. I had been trying to figure that one out for a few years. If you had asked me five years ago, I would have been certain not just of what I did, but what I planned to keep doing for as long as I could. Serve as an officer in the Indian Army. In the journey since then, I had found many things, most precious of all Zoya and Aman, but one thing that continued to elude me was peace.

Zoya was packing my clothes and she was doing her best to put on a brave face. I left Aman with his toys and went to our room, holding her from behind, nuzzling her neck.

'Major, is that your way of bribing me about your going off on another dangerous mission?'

I began to protest when she laughed. 'Well, don't stop. It was working.'

As I started to get back to what I was doing, my phone rang.

'Talk about bad timing.' When I saw that it was the sat phone, I picked it up.

It was Gopal. 'Major, we have definite information on the target's whereabouts. Your cover's in place, and I'll leave it to you to decide which plan you use. You don't need to check back with me, that would slow things down. We will have an officer there to help you, someone you already know.'

As I hung up, I tried to put the trip out of my mind and get back to Zoya. We lay together for hours, talking, touching and a part of me realized that both of us wanted to make this night last forever, because neither of us was sure what lay ahead, and whether we would have another night such as this together.

'Aadi, I've never asked you, but when you went to the Taj knowing you were the target, or earlier, when you were in the army headed out on missions, weren't you ever scared?'

I turned to face her. 'I was scared every single time,

and I was scared at the Taj. Nobody's brave all the time. The ones who survive in combat are the ones who train themselves to be a little less scared for the few seconds that matter.'

She looked at me, eyes widening in surprise. 'You never told me that. All the time I've known you, loved you, you've always seemed in control, so sure of yourself.'

'I am scared even now. Not for my own safety, but that I won't be able to come back; that the guy who killed so many and nearly killed Ravi will get away and come for you and Aman again. It was the same when I was in the army. I was scared of letting my men down, of not completing the mission. That fear is what I turn into focus, to make sure I get strength from it instead of letting it paralyse me. At the Taj, when I was walking down the alley, I was thinking of the first time we kissed, and how I wanted to get back to you.'

Zoya nuzzled closer and kissed me. 'Come back.'

'I promise I will.'

But later as I lay in the bed, I wondered if offering myself up as bait once again was the best way to stick to that promise.

'Welcome, Major!'

Sandeep Krishnan was looking as dapper as ever, and he shook my hand vigorously. Godbole was a few steps behind me. This time I thought he had not slept as well on the way and looked rather the worse for wear.

'So, Godbole, another easy one and we can grab a few drinks before you go back? What say?'

Godbole nodded listlessly as he walked towards the waiting car. Krishnan handed me something and I saw that it was a phone and a Bluetooth earpiece.

'For us to keep in touch. It's encrypted.'

'I gather cultural attachés are getting some training in using encrypted phones?'

He gave me a dirty look and got in the car.

Later that night, Godbole was drunk and had begun to snore while sitting in the hotel bar, something I would have found amusing while I nursed my Coke had Krishnan not nudged me.

'Let's get this tub of lard up to his room and you and I can talk business.'

A few minutes later, we were back at the bar and Krishnan's body language visibly changed. Gone was the languid good humour he affected. He was all business, his back straight, his eyes boring into mine. He smiled and offered me a drink, which I refused.

'Good to be rid of that corrupt babu. Now you and I can talk as professionals.'

I didn't say anything. My first experience with Krishnan hadn't exactly made a very positive impression, but if he wanted to chat, I would listen. It wasn't as if I had anything terribly exciting to do.

'He used to come to see if he could get his cut of the ransom. Randhawa stopped that by sending someone along.' At that, he raised his glass in a toast. 'To Randhawa. May he enjoy good Scotch in Heaven.'

I smiled as I raised my glass and glanced at the bottle of expensive Scotch on the table next to Krishnan. He caught my gaze. I must have let on what was on my mind.

'Major, you thought I was skimming off money with that turd?'

When I didn't say anything, he laughed out loud. 'Oh, God! I can't believe this! You thought I was like him? I can see why. Look at me, Major. A dozen years in the R&AW, straight out of a couple of years of working in the ITBP after joining the IPS; a bunch of foreign postings at embassies with lots of foreign service allowance; a ruined marriage and no kids; and now this godforsaken place with nothing to do and not much to spend my hardship allowance on other than my occasional Scotch. I may have a messed-up life, but I do not steal money from my own government.'

For the first time, I began to warm to Krishnan. I knew the lonely life that came with doing dirty work for the government, and I felt bad for him. In the army, while our work was dangerous, I had enjoyed the camaraderie of my brothers in arms. For someone like Krishnan, it was a much lonelier mission.

'I'm sorry. I didn't know all that, and my recent experience with spooks hasn't been great.'

He just shrugged and poured himself another drink. 'Here's the deal, Major. Zhang is in town. We're not sure why, but he has been spotted meeting some Vietnamese officers. For all we know, they're on the Chinese payroll and he's getting information, or, knowing his reputation, they aren't cooperating and he's here to shake them down.'

'How come the Vietnamese don't know he's here? Why not tip off their intelligence? They would be operating on home ground and would find it easier to get him.'

At that, Krishnan looked at me as if seeing me for the first time. 'Not bad, Major. Very good questions. Presumably he's operated here for some time and must have a good cover or local contacts. Also, don't overestimate the moral rectitude of Vietnamese officers or cops. It's quite likely some are on the MSS payroll and are helping Zhang. We spotted him because we were actively looking for him. If we tip the Vietnamese off, they may grab him for their own purposes, and we don't get access to him. Or if he's got inside connections, they could tip him off and he'll disappear. Plus, the MSS plays at the pro level. These aren't amateur terrorists of the sort you and I have had occasion to meet. If they feel they could be compromised, they may kill Zhang themselves. I'm sure he's good at what he does, but in our business everyone's expendable.'

I looked at the bartender and ordered a beer. Krishnan raised an eyebrow.

'I do drink, Krishnan. I just don't drink when I'm on a mission or in sight of the enemy.'

He nodded slightly and we raised a toast. As I took a sip, I asked, 'What's the plan?'

Krishnan began to laugh again, and when he spoke, I

was even more reassured. If Gopal had entrusted him with what we knew about Unit 7, I could trust him.

'Major, our world is so convoluted one day we'll feed ourselves misinformation! We've already leaked info to known MSS informants that you're here on a routine hostage recovery trip, escorting Godbole. We planted emails to the government demanding ransom for a boat and its crew that we ourselves paid some pirates to make disappear. We've planted emails from you to the office saying you didn't want to come on this trip. That was overridden as Godbole asked for you specifically. Zhang knows you saw him, so it was important to establish your hesitation. We then manufactured reports of a firefight soon after the attack on you between the cops and a man suspected of being your attacker. That culminated in a car exploding and the man being burnt beyond recognition. We had mails from Phadke's account sent to you saying the man you believed to be behind the attack at your home and near the Taj was dead and that the case is closed. The MSS will make the following assumptions. One, that we believe Zhang dead. Two, that you don't have the envelope. But they seem desperate to get the paper back, and they know Anita contacted you, so they may want to grab you to find out what you know. Your being out of India makes you a softer target, especially since Zhang is here. We know MSS has many more assets here than in India. Gopal Sir briefed me on this Unit 7, so we need to be careful.'

As I took it all in, I realized just how little I was in control. These people could hack my mail, could set me up, could save me, or could hang me out to dry. As I thought of everything Krishnan had said, I realized even he was out of the loop on one critical aspect—Karzai. Gopal was clearly playing that close to his chest. Perhaps he thought it might lead to awkwardness to let too many people know who the senior most level of the Indian government was collaborating with, or at least helping. Someone who was still wanted as a terrorist by the Americans. Wheels within wheels, and I was just a very small cog.

'So, I'm back to being the bait?'

He smiled and poured himself another drink. 'Don't look so glum, Major. Being bait is better than being the fish that's being baited.'

———————◆◆◆———————

Ho Chi Minh City was home to close to nine million souls. And, Gopal had been coy about how he expected me to bump into Karzai.

If Gopal's plan depended on me working with Karzai, I hoped he had figured out more than he had let on to me. He had asked me if I had any way of getting in touch with Karzai, and I had said no. Karzai was the kind of guy who got in touch with you. The last time I had heard from Karzai was when he had sent me a message after he had shot Ross. Then he had melted away.

Gopal had said that he would figure something out. By now, I had learned through bitter experience that when politicians, bureaucrats or spooks said they would develop a plan, it usually meant that grunts like me were going to be thrown into harm's way.

That was exactly how I felt now.

Gopal hadn't told me anything other than to go to the Apocalypse Now Bar and wait. It took barely a minute or two to be driven there in an Indian embassy car. I would have preferred to walk there in the cool winter night. Not just to enjoy the walk, but to avoid the knowing glances that the driver and Balwant, a security staffer assigned to me, gave me when I told them where I wanted to go. Gopal had told me to not take Krishnan along and refused me permission to walk.

'No, we don't want Zhang to come for you. Not yet anyway.'

When I entered the bar, I realized just why the driver had been smirking at me and asking me how long I expected to be there. Yes, it was a bar, but it seemed selling drinks was not the only, and certainly not the most visible, sort of business it did. Lining the bar, and draped across its many couches, were women. Women who smiled as I came in, and no, not because of my charming good looks, but because they smelled a potential customer in me.

What the hell was Gopal thinking? My phone rang. Zoya was trying to FaceTime me. Going undercover isn't as glamorous as the movies make it out to be. In my case, it meant not accepting a video call because there was no way I could explain to Zoya what sort of mission had brought me into a bar where I was surrounded by prostitutes. So I did the only thing that came to mind—I accepted it as an audio call.

'Aadi, why didn't you accept my video call?'

'Hi, Zo, the signal's not too good, so I wasn't sure the video would work.'

I'm good at some things, but lying isn't one of them. While I could refuse to turn on the video, it was impossible to blank out the music blaring in the background.

'The major seems to be hard at work at midnight, with that music playing around. Don't work too hard.'

Ouch! When you're trapped between a spook and a wife, always pick the wife. So I did the only thing I could and told Zo a version of the truth—the only version I could give over an open line that was probably being tapped. I'd give her the full story later.

'Just thought I'd get a drink. Tomorrow is going to be such a bore. God knows why they send me for these jobs.'

'Well, don't drink too much and get some sleep.'

That was harder said than done, as I sat there nursing a beer with woman after woman coming up to me and asking me if I wanted some fun. When the fourth woman came to me, laying her hand on my thigh, I decided I'd had enough and leaned towards her. She smiled in anticipation, which dissipated as soon as the next words left my mouth.

'I'm sorry, but I'm gay.'

She walked away, but that was not the end of my torment, for word clearly spread and the next companion I had was a ladyboy.

'Gay? Maybe you like me? I both boy and girl. Two in one.'

I decided I was going to shoot Gopal when I next met

him. My thoughts of revenge were put on hold when a boy who had been serving snacks handed me a note.

Major, meet me in the bathroom. Seven Six Two.

All other thoughts disappeared. Karzai was here! I went to the bathroom and saw it was unoccupied, save a man whistling inside one of the toilet cubicles. I walked to the door. 'Is that you?'

The door opened and I found myself facing Aman Karzai. His hair greyer than I remembered, but otherwise he was in great shape. When I had last met him, he had seemed to have lost weight, but now he was back to the wiry, muscular build I had seen in Mumbai, his slightly wry grin there, and his eyes ablaze as they bored into me.

'You are a fool, Major. This is a nest of vipers and they will strike you down before you even know what you're doing.'

I had no idea what Karzai knew or what Gopal and gang had fed him, so I asked what he knew.

'I know Zhang is alive, and I know he's here. I also know he knows you're here.' Before I could say anything else, he pulled me into the cubicle and closed the door. 'Major, this is crazy for me to even be here. I have been going about my business, but as I got on this man's trail, I learned he was in Afghanistan when Project Lotus was on, and helped set up the drone strike that killed my family. I've traced him here and would have taken him out, but I learned he knew you were here and was going to get you.'

I saw this man before me, a man who lived by a simple code of honour, because of which he had risked a lot to try to warn me. A man who had once put his own life on the line to save my family. I decided then that spooks be damned, I would be straight with him.

I told him everything. When I finished, he looked at me appraisingly.

'I've said this to you before, Major. You are either very brave or just insane.'

'I am neither, Karzai. This bastard has caused so much pain to so many people, and he came after my family. Just as you, I have a score to settle with him. I really don't give a shit about codes on a paper, but I care about the fact that a man, perhaps a man like you and me, is lying in a cell somewhere, beaten, tortured, and forgotten by those he served.'

We heard noises outside and I opened the door to see the ladyboy outside. He (or is it she?) winked at me and I shook my head. When Karzai's head appeared next to me, the ladyboy pouted at me.

'What does he have that I don't? I will call the manager and tell you fooling around here.'

I had dealt with jihadis in Kashmir, guns for hire in Mumbai and Chechen torturers in Afghanistan, but nothing had prepared me for what happened next.

Karzai stepped out. 'Tell him there is a bomb here and I will blow you all up. Allahu Akbar!'

Then many things happened in quick succession. The ladyboy shrieked and ran back into the bar. We heard the patrons running and shouting and the sounds of furniture being toppled. Karzai ran out the bathroom, asking me to follow him.

We ran, not to the front door, but to the back, through the kitchen, where Karzai took out a grenade from his pocket and as we exited the door lobbed it back into the kitchen. We ran for our lives, diving behind a parked car as the grenade exploded, throwing the door off its hinges, shattering windows on parked cars and setting a large part of the building on fire.

'What the fuck did you do that for?'

I'd thought I was the impulsive, crazy one among us. Karzai had always been cool, contemplative and grounded, and here he was, going Rambo on me! He grinned at me.

'Just run, and I'll tell you.'

With that, he took off in a fast, loping gait that I struggled to keep up with. In a stand-up fight, I could have bested him, but he was built like a marathon runner and could run me into the ground. But I was stubborn and proud and wouldn't let it show how tough it was to keep up with him, so I did my best. However, talking while running was beyond me, so I was happy he was doing all the talking.

'I'm sure Unit 7 is watching you. That fire is a good distraction. Also, the owner of that bar is an arms dealer who wanted me to burn it down to get insurance money. Seems he invested dirty money into opening the bar and he has great insurance cover. This helps him launder some of that dirty money. My payment to get access to the bar to meet you.'

Every time I thought I met the wrong sorts of people in my previous line of work, Karzai showed me just how cocooned my life was compared to his. He kept running into a darkened alley and then into a waiting car and beckoned me to follow.

As I sat inside and the car sped off, Karzai smiled at me. 'Now, Major, we can plan how to take down this bastard Zhang without all the spooks watching you.'

'Where are we going?'

'You'll find out soon. Welcome to my world, Major.'

The room was small but spotlessly clean and well lit. Karzai and I were sitting on chairs around a small table in the middle of the room and he had a tattered map of the city open in front of us.

'Major, tell me are you just suicidal or do the Indians hate your guts so much that they dangle you out as bait all the time?'

He had said it with a smile, but I could see his eyes hardening.

'They came after my family. They were waiting inside our home. Me, I get. God knows I've had men want to kill me before, but Aman and Zoya? They killed an innocent woman who only wanted to do the right thing; they killed my boss; and they almost killed the closest thing to a father I have. So nobody's dangling me as bait. I'm hunting these bastards.'

He didn't say anything for a while.

'Major, in all the time I've known you, I've seen you angry, but whoever these idiots are, they have pissed you off more than ever. I pity them. I know from personal experience just how little fun it is to have you hunt someone.'

He grinned, leaving unsaid the fact that we had first crossed paths when he had sworn to kill me and I had taken him to be a deadly enemy. How far we had come from those days. Now, he was a man I trusted and saw as a comrade no less reliable than the buddies I had served with in uniform. Part of me felt guilty at having what most people would consider a normal life—a family, a job—while he lived his life in the shadows, waging a lonely war out of a sense of honour that I could only bring myself to admire, but never imagine following.

'What's on your mind, Major? You seem lost in thought.'

'What keeps you going, Karzai? Why don't you just melt away and settle down somewhere?'

He smiled, but I could see the sadness in his eyes. 'I tried doing that, remember? Perhaps it's my curse that whenever I try to find peace, violence seeks me out. I would like to turn away, but I remember something my father used to tell me. In the world, there are three kinds of people—sheep, wolves and sheepdogs. He said no son of his would ever be a sheep who blindly followed others or a wolf who preyed on the weak. So I have no option but to be the sheep dog.'

I clapped him on the shoulder. 'That is not a curse. It is a gift your father has given you.'

He tipped his head. His grin was back. 'So, will we chat like old gossips, or actually talk about how to keep you alive tomorrow?'

'What's your plan? Moreover, how are you planning to pull it off here? Isn't this very far from your usual hunting grounds?'

Karzai brought me up to speed. Some of the files and disks he had managed to get out of the base in Afghanistan had led him to Ross. They also showed that Ross was a cog in the wheel—an important cog, but the real driving force of that machine had something to do with the Chinese.

'I tapped into a bunch of old contacts—people now in private security—and after some time, I managed to get a hit. One of my old Russian trainers is a bodyguard for a Russian tycoon. Turns out one of his colleagues is Chinese and served in their special forces. When I asked him to find out more, he got back saying his pal had been approached for a job in Afghanistan. The man who approached him sounded a lot like Zhang. I'm sure there are others above Zhang, but he keeps popping up when I trace the people behind Lotus. I've been on his trail for some time, and recently, I got a tip-off from some contacts that he was here.'

'Where does this all lead? I mean I would be happy to just be left alone, and maybe get some payback for all that they have done. What's your endgame?'

I saw a haunted look in Karzai's eyes as he answered. 'Major, I am a dead man. I died when I held Arfa's body in my arms after she killed herself, unable to live with the shame of being raped by those American contractors. I died again when I had to pick up the pieces of what remained when my mother and family were killed in a drone strike. Unlike you, I have no life to go back to. I just have a duty to fulfil before I can rejoin Arfa and my mother. A duty to avenge them. When we learned Karimi was one of the brains behind Lotus and had engineered the drone strike, he was a dead man. When we learned that it was Ross' men who had raped Arfa, he was a dead man. When I learned about Zhang and his masters, they were dead men too.'

I looked at Karzai, a man capable of being honourable, yet one who could be a ruthless killer. To most people, that might seem a contradiction. But to me, it was a glimpse into my own soul. Sure, on the face of it, I had a 'normal' life compared to Karzai, but now, meeting him again, I realized that we were more alike than different.

'Karzai, you sell yourself short. It's not just revenge you care about. Hanif's doing well, my friend. Rachel sent me photos and videos. He's in a good school and well settled in the US.'

Hanif was the boy who had accompanied me and Karzai in Afghanistan, a boy whom Karzai had vowed would not grow up with the violence he had. Rachel Harmening, the daughter of the former US President and the hostage we had helped rescue, had taken Hanif under her wing.

Karzai's response shocked me as he smiled. 'Yes, she sent me those as well.'

For a second, I stared at him in disbelief. The elusive sniper hunted by many enemies was in touch with Rachel. In Afghanistan, surrounded by enemies, I had thought I had spotted a connection. At the time, I had laughed it off as my imagination, perhaps there was something to it. I saw the glint in Karzai's eyes as he continued.

'She is a remarkable woman, and understands what I am doing. She may not always approve, but she understands. As I uncover information, I send a lot back to her. Being the journalist who broke Ross' nexus and with the kind of access she has, she can be very helpful.'

Now my mind was spinning. So Rachel was helping him in his quest!

'I've been sharing the information with her. I know I can't hunt all of them myself, so if she can help as a journalist or by getting the information to the US government, I'm fine. Just two threads of information that I haven't shared with her.'

'What are those?'

'First, links to Zhang and the Chinese. I'm happy if the Americans take out arms dealers and bankers in Pakistan and the Middle East, but the Chinese seem to be running the show. I'm going after them myself. I got my hands on an external hard drive that I wasn't able to access. The hackers I got it to said it had military-grade encryption. I figure that drive has something really important on it and am waiting to get hold of someone in the Chinese hierarchy to figure out what's on it. All my guy could decode was one name, the title of the disk.'

'What was that?'

'Camel.'

Where had I heard that name before? With everything that had happened, it was hard to place it, but I could swear that name had popped up earlier.

'Now, Major, shall we get on with talking about tomorrow?'

The map in front of me had all kinds of notations on it, and if there was something I had come to learn about Karzai it was that he had in spades the skill that all great snipers need. Patience. So if he was as confident as he seemed, he had a plan that might just work.

'Major, I hope this Krishnan is as competent as you think. Just the two of us will have no chance against Zhang and his men when they come after you.'

'He seems to know his stuff, and this mission was sanctioned directly by the prime minister and Gopal, so I'm assuming he will have access to the resources he needs. I presume you will work the usual magic with your rifle. I know you want to kill Zhang, but if we want to get to the bottom of what's going on and also to rescue the man the Chinese have, it will be better to get him alive. I won't ask you to not shoot him, but try to take out his men and let Krishnan and his team get Zhang alive.'

I could see Karzai think that over in silence. Finally, he took a deep breath and exhaled. 'I don't care about the plans of spies and governments, Indian or Chinese. But if there's a soldier whose life may be saved by getting Zhang alive, I can understand that. But I have a condition.'

'What?'

'If the Indians get Zhang, you need to tell me everything they find out.'

'Karzai, I'm just a foot soldier. Do you think the government will tell me all the secrets they find out?'

He looked at me, his eyes boring into mine. 'I don't care about Chinese geopolitical plans. I just care about who else beyond Zhang was involved in Lotus.'

'I'll tell you what I can find out. Now what do you need me to do?'

He smiled, his eyes twinkling. 'Do what your Indian bosses so love making you do—be the bait. This time, I have some toys of my own I'd like to give you. Toys the late Mister Ross is paying for with his ill-earned money.'

Godbole joined me the next morning over breakfast, looking much the worse for wear.

'Morning. Looks like you still haven't gotten over your jet lag.'

He mumbled something about being tired and having problems sleeping and proceeded to stuff his plate. His hangdog expression indicated that the number of drinks he had put into himself had more to do with his condition than any jet lag. I picked at the omelette on my plate, thinking about the day ahead, while Godbole wolfed down eggs and enough slices of French toast to feed a small army and washed it all down with three cups of tea. Just when I thought he was done, he got up to fetch some cake. He offered me some, but I politely declined. Godbole had no idea what was actually going on, and thought he was really there on another hostage exchange. The hostage pick-up, a pure piece of fiction engineered by Krishnan's bosses, was the next day. This morning, I was to accompany Godbole to a more or less routine meeting with some Vietnamese company. He would be attending the meeting, while I, essentially little more than a bodyguard, would get the day off to play tourist.

That was when Krishnan was betting that Zhang would come for me. And I was betting that with Karzai helping out, we would have the element of surprise over him.

I tried to act the tourist. It was more fun than I'd thought. I visited Ho Chi Minh's Mausoleum and then the Military History Museum, where I spent over an hour looking at hardware left over from the Vietnam war and exhibits and photos of another war where politicians had decided they needed to go to war, sitting in comfortable rooms and looking at clean maps, which didn't expose them to the fact that the real ground the maps represented was covered with the blood of young soldiers. The reasons changed—ideology, land, oil, or sometimes nothing more than the fact that leaders didn't like each other. The result was always the same—some died, and others had to learn to live with what they had become. Nobody went to war and came back the same as who they had been before.

I saw a photo of a Viet Cong soldier emerging out of a tunnel, and I looked into his eyes. Young, confident, but with an empty, haunted look that comes with having seen more death and suffering than any human being should. A look I knew well. A look I saw every time I looked at myself in the mirror.

My roaming around all by myself given what had happened recently in Mumbai might have been suspicious, but Gopal had that covered as well. His spooks had manufactured chatter about how they knew I was travelling but had no significant assets to assign to me in Vietnam. The MSS would have known as much, but Gopal was not leaving any stone unturned. He had also had the IB send an internal memo through what he termed 'known vulnerable' internal channels about the security arrangements for me while in Vietnam—namely, a single embassy security staffer, and no specific security when I went for the hostage pickup, when I would be surrounded by armed Vietnamese troops. I had not commented on it, but I didn't know whether to be worried that the country's intelligence head knew that internal communications in the IB were compromised or to be impressed that he knew and was using it to deliberately feed misinformation.

The security staffer, a glum-looking Sikh called Balwant, didn't look so happy about accompanying me. That was the whole point of this exercise.

'Balwant, I still have some time to kill. Fancy a walk?'

I could tell he hardly fancied it, but had no real option but to follow me. The plan was for me to broadcast my location to Krishnan over my mobile phone, which the spooks were sure the MSS was tapping. Before I could make that call, my phone rang. It was Godbole.

'My meeting finished early. I'm just stepping out for a sec. My wife insisted I pick up some silks, so am going to the Silk Market at Hang Gai Street. Why don't you meet me there?'

Shit. As usual with best-laid plans, things hardly played out by the script. I called Krishnan on the encrypted phone. After he let loose a few choice profanities, he composed himself. 'Our snatch teams were waiting near the lake where you were supposed to be. I guess they can be there at the Silk Market within fifteen minutes, but I don't like going in unprepared. Too many things could go wrong.'

'Where's Zhang?'

'Still very much here. I have an asset watching him. He's no more than a klick from the lake. We were confident he would make a move when you were walking around the lake. I'm pretty sure he has assets watching you as well.'

I thought it over. 'He won't come out tomorrow when I have Vietnamese soldiers around. Today's our only chance. Let's improvise. I'll get there but get your men there ASAP.'

Karzai had given me another mobile phone to stay in touch, and I sent him a message. He replied with a laconic, 'Trust the bureaucrats to fuck up.' I smiled as I read his reply and knew that even if Krishnan's team took time, Karzai would get there faster. Knowing he would have my back was a far better prospect than heading into unfamiliar territory all on my own.

I told Balwant about the change of plans and we got into the embassy car as I headed off on a trip where success essentially amounted to my being attacked.

Talk about a truly messed-up definition of success.

I wasn't sure what I had expected, but the moment I stepped into the five-hundred-metre or so stretch of road called the Silk Market, I knew it was a tourist trap. Shops lined both sides of the street, some larger establishments and some small roadside stalls, all peddling clothes and crafts made of fine silk. It was colourful, that much I'd be willing to grant, as the street seemed to be swathed in hues of vibrant colours.

I called Godbole to check where he was.

'Just keep going down the street. You'll pass a Buddhist temple on your left, and then take the next left turn. There's a bakery there, where I'm having a coffee.'

'Okay. I'm wearing a black cap and dark jeans and a t-shirt. Given how crowded this place is, watch out for me in case I miss the bakery.'

Godbole sounded out of breath, and I wondered how unfit he was if a walk down this market had left him so winded.

When I called Krishnan, he chuckled when he heard where Godbole was. 'The fat bastard's probably stuffing his face with cake. Okay, Major, the game is on. I had a team shadowing you, and you picked up a tail soon after you left.'

As I began to instinctively turn to see who was following me, Krishnan cut in, as if reading my mind. 'Don't look for him. You may give the game away. Zhang is going to make his move soon, and I'm not too far away.'

'I hope you've brought enough men and guns. Zhang isn't an amateur.'

'Don't worry, Major. The US dollar buys all kinds of services. We have two separate teams of mercenaries there to run interference and my own team to snatch Zhang.'

As I put the phone back in my pocket, I couldn't help but smile. Krishnan and his bosses at the R&AW clearly were bringing their best game, and that reassured me a bit. That, and the fact that my own guardian angel, Karzai, was surely around somewhere, peering down his scope to take out anyone who could threaten me. It's at moments like that when you realize who you can really trust. For all that Gopal had told me and for all of Krishnan's swagger, I realized that when the shit hit the fan, there was one man I knew I could count on. Karzai.

Balwant was walking behind me, clearly not happy to be in a crowded market when he had been told that he was to watch over me because of a security threat. I passed a shop with a colourful board with the name 'Life is Shirt'. I turned left just ahead of that shop and could see the sign for the bakery fifty metres away.

Godbole was on the street, and he waved to me. I waved back and began to walk towards him. The phone Karzai had given me buzzed.

I could sense the urgency in Karzai's voice as I answered. 'Major, I don't like the look of things. Get out of there. Get out now!'

Karzai's warning came way too late. A second later, things went to hell.

I heard a screeching noise behind me and Balwant screamed, a primal shout of pain and shock. I turned and saw him on the ground, a pool of blood spreading around him, his legs crushed by the SUV that had slammed into him. Four men dressed in black, wearing masks were getting out, all of them carrying assault rifles. I had met such enemies before in Afghanistan. They were likely commandos of Unit 7, and their arrival meant that well before we were ready to spring our trap, Zhang had made his move.

I walked up to Balwant and saw he was already dead. I fished inside his jacket, grabbed the gun he had and then ran towards Godbole. I could hear heavy boots behind me. At least they were not shooting. Some comfort. At least that meant Zhang wanted me alive. If they had wanted to kill me, I would have already been dead.

I careened into Godbole and pulled him behind a large ice-cream freezer. His eyes were wide with fear. The moment I saw them, I knew something was wrong. He was shocked at the sudden violence, but didn't seem surprised. For a desk-bound bureaucrat like him to not be more rattled at what had happened was not normal. Then things clicked into place—he was the one who had called me here. The greedy pig had set me up.

'What have you done, you bastard?'

He was shaking as I grabbed his neck. 'I'm sorry, Major. They promised me they would not kill anyone.'

I fumbled in my pocket to call Krishnan but put my phone back when automatic weapon fire exploded in the street around us. Krishnan and his men were presumably coming to the rescue. A couple of bullets ricocheted off the wall to our left and Godbole howled in fright.

'This wasn't supposed to happen. They said they would just take a package from you. They offered to pay me...'

I backhanded him across his face and the shock of the sudden blow, more than the force with which it had been delivered, shut him up.

I flicked the safety off Balwant's pistol and leaned out from the side of the freezer. All four of my pursuers were behind the SUV, trading fire with gunmen I couldn't see. They were well hidden and firing like professionals, carefully aimed single shots or bursts of three from the Kalashnikovs, not 'spraying and praying' like many jihadis I'd been up against. While they had good cover from Krishnan's men, they were open to me. I took aim and fired twice. I didn't think I hit anyone, but as I ducked back, several bullets slammed against the freezer. I didn't stand much of a chance with a pistol against four trained men with assault rifles, but perhaps I could distract them a bit while help came.

Where was Karzai?

That question was answered when one of the men fell, his head exploding from a direct hit. The other three cowered behind the SUV again. One of them raised his head to see where the shot had come from. That was the last thing he did, as a shot took him in the neck and he fell dead. His two remaining comrades leaned out from behind cover and began firing at me. There was too much incoming fire to do much else other than take cover. However, in those few seconds I realized they had not yet registered that there was another shooter on one of the rooftops near us. They probably thought I had shot the two men Karzai had taken out. If these four guys were all that had been sent to grab me, then between Karzai on the roof, me behind cover, and Krishnan's men coming to help, our chances of getting away were high. But it also meant that we had blown our chances of getting Zhang. I knew the man I could blame for that and when Godbole whimpered something about whether we would get out alive, I took my frustration out on him and slapped him again, sending him crashing against the side of the freezer. To my disgust, the bastard began weeping like a child. I was sorely tempted to blow his brains out, but realized explaining that would be a bit hard when and if I did manage to get out of this alive.

I heard a dull thump, followed by the sound of something metallic bouncing off a wall, and then a loud explosion. Then it happened again. It was a sound I knew well, though it was hard to believe that a bustling market was being turned into a war zone in the middle of the day. If these guys had under-barrel grenade launchers attached to their assault rifles, then it was likely Krishnan's men were seriously outgunned. The phone Krishnan had given me rang.

As I picked it up, I could hear the tension in Krishnan's voice. 'Major, they were ready for us. They ambushed us at multiple points and tore our men apart. They just took out our reinforcements with grenades. I'm coming in with a small squad, but we're badly outnumbered and outgunned. Hang in there. I'm calling the Vietnamese to help—am sure the cops are on the way now, anyway.'

I wanted to tell him that hanging in there wasn't really an option for me, it was the only one. I couldn't really fight my way out, and I didn't see an easy escape. I looked behind me and spotted a small alley some twenty metres away. Maybe if I ran fast enough, maybe if they really were under orders not to kill me, I might make it. I got up in a crouch and dove behind a table as two men with assault rifles came out of the alley and knelt, aiming at us.

I heard several more bursts of gunfire, and then two more grenades being fired. A brief silence, followed by two loud bursts that I knew were fragmentation grenades. A brief lull. Then a single shot.

The battle was over, and I had a bad feeling about who had won. Krishnan and his reinforcements were not likely to be coming. My attackers were now quiet, perhaps waiting for their own reinforcements.

The phone Karzai had given me rang. 'Major, I saw multiple teams converge on the area. I tried to warn you, but it was too late.'

'Karzai, what's done is done. Looks like we were all taken by surprise.'

'I can see more men coming over from the alley. I'll try to take out as many as I can.'

'No, Karzai. Sounds like there are too many of them, and they have too much firepower. Not much you can do. Get away. It's me they are after.'

'I'm sorry, Major. I won't leave a brother behind.'

There was nothing to be said after that. Karzai and I had seen a lot together, but if it was to all end here, in this alley far from either of our homes, it was some comfort that I would not be facing it alone.

'Major, they'll be here any minute. I don't think they know I'm here so I'll try to keep that element of surprise for as long as I can.'

I knew what was coming and I called Zoya. 'Hi, sweetheart.'

'Aadi, everything okay? Are you coming back tomorrow?'

'Zo, they may need me for a few more days. Listen, I love you and Aman more than anything else in the world, and I'll do my best to get back soon.'

When she responded after a brief pause, I could hear her voice catch. 'Aadi, please tell me you're okay.'

'Zo, you know me. I'm just too damned stubborn to be kept away from you for long. Kiss Aman for me.'

As I hung up, I wondered if I'd ever see my family again.

The phone rang and I picked it up, hopeful that somehow, against the odds, Krishnan had survived and there was still hope. It wasn't him on the other end of the line, but a voice I had heard before, speaking in accented English.

'Major, all your friends are dead. Surrender now. You don't have to die, and we have no intention of killing you needlessly. I would prefer to take you alive.'

Zhang. The fact that he had Krishnan's phone confirmed my fears that the man was dead. I put the phone down and weighed my options.

'Can you fight your way out?'

I had forgotten Godbole was there, and in response to his asinine question, I slapped him again. I really felt like shooting him.

'You are a fucking idiot. Krishnan and God know how many more are dead because of you. As for me fighting my way out, what do you think this is? A movie? And who do you think I am? Jason Bourne? James fucking Bond?'

He began to say something and out of sheer frustration, I slapped him again. To my surprise he began to cry once again. I looked up and saw four masked men coming towards me, moving from cover to cover like trained soldiers. The two men behind me were in their original positions, cutting off the only escape route I had. I didn't have too many options, but I was damned if I was going to make this easy.

The men coming towards me were good, but getting complacent, thinking they had this wrapped up. One took a fraction longer moving to his next cover than he would have had he been in combat, and I put two bullets in him. As he fell, his comrades hunkered down and began pouring fire on my position. The two men behind me also got into the act, and with bullets flying around me, I had no option but to lie down flat.

The firing stopped, and the phone rang again.

It was Zhang once again. 'Major, you do not have to die. You don't have much on your side. Bullets, weapons, men. Nothing.'

'I do have time, Zhang.'

As he hung up, I could almost picture him thinking it through. The cops would be here anytime, and I doubted Zhang and his men would want to slaughter them in the middle of the city. Whatever plan they had to get away must have hinged on getting to me fast and melting away. Having to battle Krishnan's men had already delayed them, and if I could just be a pain in the ass and hold them up a bit longer, I might just come out of this.

Then something truly remarkable happened. Six more uniformed men joined the three remaining ones from the SUV and began running towards me. Smart call by Zhang, but a ruthless one. I thought back to accounts I had read of Indian army officers who had faced the Chinese army in 1962. They would report Chinese 'human waves' of hundreds, even thousands of soldiers rushing Indian positions. The Indian Army often inflicted a terrible toll but were overwhelmed by sheer numbers. I had read about the same tactic being used in the Korean War by the Chinese against the Americans. Now I was facing my own little version of that. I had only a handful of bullets. I fired five carefully aimed shots, seeing two men going down before my pistol clicked: empty.

That was when Karzai opened up. One man went down, a spray of blood coming from his neck. His comrades stopped, bewildered. That hesitation cost another man his life as Karzai shot him in the head. The others took cover and began firing at the roof, and I was left to watch in frustration, with no bullets left and unable to help Karzai. He had told me he would not leave me behind, and he was true to his word. Another man fell to his bullet, but these were trained soldiers, and knew they were up against a concealed sniper, they took cover and called in reinforcements. Two men crept up, and I saw the large tubular barrels attached to their assault rifles, through which they could launch grenades.

I called Karzai. 'They have UBGLs. Get out of there!'

The two masked men fired almost at the same time, the grenades arcing up towards the roof. The two explosions, a split second apart, sent pieces of masonry, windows and furniture flying around me. I had curled myself up into a ball to avoid the debris as best as I could, but I was cut in several places from the flying glass. Godbole had neither the training nor the common sense to take cover and was bleeding from a horrible-looking gash on his forehead and making a keening noise. I screamed in frustration as I realized that Karzai had perhaps been killed trying to protect me.

It felt like an eternity, but it was perhaps a few seconds. My attackers waited to see if there was anyone still shooting from the roof, a couple of them moving out from cover to a new location. I kept hoping the fabled sniper codenamed Seven Six Two would cheat death, but there were no more shots from the roof.

Six men now ran towards my position. I stood up, facing them as they came. The first man to reach me paid for his over-enthusiasm as I swept his feet from under him and stomped him in the neck with my steel-tipped boots. The next man swung his rifle butt towards my head like a club. I ducked and launched myself at him, bringing my head up against his nose. As his nose broke, he seemed to crumple. For all my efforts, the result of the fight was a foregone conclusion.

As I said, I wasn't Jason Bourne and this was no movie. The remaining men waded into me with a flurry of kicks, punches and blows from their rifle butts. They had me down, bloodied and bruised in a minute, and my hands tied behind my back. They ran with me towards the back alley as I began to hear approaching sirens. One of them was also dragging Godbole along.

As we reached the alley, a man stepped out, wearing black, a scar across his cheek. I knew that face well. It was Zhang.

'Hello, Major. Looks like you enjoy doing things the hard way.'

'Looks like you need an army to get me. Scared of trying one on one again? Or did getting your ass kicked convince you that you needed all these men to come after me?'

His eyes hardened and Godbole picked absolutely the worst moment he could have chosen to butt into the conversation. 'Let me go. I've done all I said I would. I had no idea there would be so much bloodshed.'

Zhang looked at him as if studying a distasteful insect, then whipped out a pistol and shot Godbole in the head. He turned and ran down the alley and his men dragged me along. I was pushed into the back of an SUV that sped off, while a handful of Zhang's men took position and began firing at the approaching Vietnamese policemen. Krishnan, I, Gopal and everyone else involved had totally underestimated just how ruthless Zhang and his masters could be, and we had all paid the price.

Zhang sat in the front of the SUV next to the driver and I was in the back, sandwiched between two armed men. He caught one man's eyes in the rear-view mirror, and the man reached into the seat pocket in front of him, took out a syringe and plunged it into my arm. In a matter of seconds, I felt my eyes closing.

Then there was darkness.

When I came to my senses, I was lying on a bare metal cot over-enthusiasm. As I tried to get up, I sat down heavily, still feeling very groggy. Whatever drug they had put into me had been potent. I was in a small room with no other furniture visible. The door to my cell swung open and Zhang stepped in with two men armed with assault rifles.

I knew my official welcome was about to begin.

A man outside handed Zhang a folding plastic chair and he sat in front of me, no more than a couple of feet away. 'So, Major, I guess you know what we want to know?'

'What?'

He actually smiled, as if he had expected me to be more defiant. 'Are you going to make this easy or hard?'

I looked into his eyes. This man had condemned several of his men to death just to get me. I had no doubt he would subject me to whatever torture he could conjure up to get what they wanted. I stayed silent and could see that Zhang was losing his patience.

'Major, I believe you have something of ours? Let me know where it is kept.'

'What the fuck are you talking about?' I hadn't even tried to be offensive. I blurted out the words in genuine surprise. I had no idea what Zhang was talking about. I never saw the blow coming and my head was rocked back when Zhang struck me with an open palm.

'Do you take me for a fool? I went to your house and couldn't find what we were looking for. If I had found it then we wouldn't need all the extra drama to get you to come to us.'

I looked at him again, assessing his eyes. He was a cool customer, but I could be a real pain in the ass. Under normal circumstances, it wasn't one of my most endearing qualities, but then being tied up in a secret Chinese facility on foreign soil didn't really count as normal.

'Drama? You killed good people and almost killed Ravi. All to get a bloody note?'

Before I could say more, he struck me again. I could taste the blood in my mouth now. I was still watching his eyes. As he leaned forward, I spat into his face, my spittle and blood splattering across his cheeks. He roared and got to his feet, kicking me down and then pummelling me with several blows before he stepped back. It hurt like hell, but when I managed to sit back up, I was smiling.

One of Zhang's men handed him a handkerchief and he used it to clean off his face. 'You find this amusing? Maybe you'll be smiling when my men pull out your fingernails.'

I was in some serious pain. My ribs hurt when I forced

a laugh, but laugh I did, just to get a rise out of him. 'No need for that, Zhang. You were a soldier once, perhaps trained like I was. Since then, you've gotten yourself mixed up in dirty business, but I assume you remember some of that training. When it comes to pulling out fingernails and other such fun pastimes, nobody holds up. Everyone sings, it's just a matter of how long. I quite like my fingernails, so I'll spare you the effort and me the pain.'

I could see him genuinely puzzled, perhaps wondering if I'd lost my mind.

'Of course, I've read the note, you idiot. I know you had an Indian prisoner here. The man who wrote it was a better man and a better soldier than you ever will be.'

'Where is it now?'

'I presume in the office of the prime minister of India.'

Now I could see panic in his eyes, and I pressed home whatever little advantage I had. 'They know it all. I was sent here to set you up, just like in Mumbai. You're good at getting out of traps, but the Indian government knows everything. It's a matter of time before they act on it and do whatever it is that they have in mind. I'm small fry here—nothing more than bait. You idiots didn't even check me for transmitters. One of your goons groped me around a bit, but do you think they'd send me with wires that even kids could find? You may fancy yourself to be an assassin, but you have a long way to go in terms of learning some tradecraft.'

As his eyes narrowed, I went on quite enjoying the tale I was spinning. Maybe I had spent too much time with spooks, but I was having fun making up a story somewhat anchored in the truth. Yes, I had seen the note, and yes, it was with the prime minister, and indeed, I was the bait. However, the Indians had put no transmitter on me and had no idea where I was. But that bluff might well help me survive a bit longer, or so I hoped.

Zhang looked ready to hit me again but stayed his hand in mid-air. 'Where is the transmitter, or do I have to cut you open?'

'It was in my mouth and dissolves into the bloodstream. The latest American technology, or so I'm told. No point killing me. They know where I am by now.'

He looked at me and I held his gaze. I had nothing to lose so was happy to bullshit along, hoping it prolonged my life long enough to figure out more about what had happened to the Indian prisoner.

'Are you telling the truth?'

I smiled. 'Look at me, Zhang. What fucking cards do I hold? Why would I lie? At best, if you see I'm just a bloody pawn, you may let me live. If you want to kill me, you'll do it anyway. Why the fuck would a man in my position lie?'

He exhaled in exasperation as he spread his palms out wide and then, to my shock and surprise, he began to laugh. 'You are a good soldier. I'll grant you that. The moment you saw a comrade in distress, the moment people you admired were killed, you were ready to put yourself in harm's way. Without even thinking of what you might be getting into. We don't give a damn about the note, Major. Ideally, we would have got what we wanted in your home. When we found nothing there, we kept reeling you in till you got here. Getting the Indian government involved makes things a bit more complicated, but nothing my bosses can't manage. In a way, it turned out well, because they sent you to us, chasing me. If the Indian government does know you're here, too bad for you, because we'll just have to speed things up before we leave.'

He laughed again. 'Imagine—you thought you were hunting me!'

'You talk too much, Zhang. When you got the chance, you couldn't do jackshit. Every time you've come up against me, I've kicked your ass, so don't pretend you've beaten me.'

His eyes hardened, but he didn't hit me again. Instead, he stormed out of the room, shouting to his men in Chinese. I wondered if he had just asked them to kill me and braced myself. Instead of shooting me, they dragged me out, through a corridor, and into a larger room. One of them cut the rope binding my hands behind me and pushed me into the room, locking it behind me.

The room was dark, dingy and would have looked right at home in a B-grade horror movie where the budget for furniture and special effects had run out and they had found the smelliest, dirtiest room in the city to shoot in instead. The only light was provided by a small ceiling lamp, and there were four wretched-looking men there. As they spoke among themselves, I guessed they were Vietnamese, since I heard a few words I thought I had heard in Vietnam, though my language skills hardly allowed me to distinguish between Vietnamese and Chinese.

One of them, a gap-toothed old man wearing torn rags, smiled at me. 'English?'

I nodded. He beamed even more, shooting off more rapid-fire phrases at his friends. Then he addressed me. 'We from boat. Welcome.'

I sat opposite the group. The room stank of all kinds of things I didn't really want to know the details of. The men themselves didn't look or smell like they had taken a bath in days. But it was nice to meet someone who didn't want to torture or kill me.

'Are you sailors? From Vietnam?'

It took a couple of repetitions and some hand gestures, but he got it and nodded. That brought a sense of relief. If Zhang had dumped me with hostages picked up from ships in the area, they would likely ransom us all. Part of me dared to think that I could actually go home to Zoya and Aman after all.

'So, they'll free us, right? When your company or government pays ransom?'

The word 'ransom' was way too tough to explain and so I had to mime handing out money.

'You'll go home when the pirates get money, right?'

At that the gap-toothed man's smile disappeared. 'Poor fisherman. No money.'

I didn't like where this was headed. Even if I wasn't willing to think through the implications of what he'd said, he went ahead and spelled it for me.

'Welcome. We all dead.' He made a gun with his fingers, pointed it at his head and laughed. 'Bang, bang!'

Dinner was a bowl of unidentifiable, watery broth, which I slurped down. One of the men, a young lad, kicked his bowl aside, muttering something that I had no doubt consisted of the choicest obscenities targeted at our captors. I looked at the old man, whom I'd taken to be their leader, spokesperson, or at least the only one among them able or willing to communicate with me. He nodded. So, I finished the second bowl. After that, as the four men watched me in something akin to horror, I stretched out on the hard floor and slept.

When I woke, two of them were still sitting, struggling to stay awake, the young man was thrashing about in his sleep, and the old man was still watching me.

I could see the look in his eyes, and I smiled at him. 'Good morning.'

'Morning. I sleep but bad. These are bad men. They pick us up because we see base.'

If these poor fishermen had stumbled onto Zhang's base, then it was indeed bad news for them. I wondered why Zhang's men hadn't just killed them outright.

The old man must have read my thoughts because he shrugged. 'They think we government spy. Beat us to see if we are. Now they know we poor fishermen. Now they kill us.'

Shit. But I had to admire his courage to stay calm knowing what was coming. When my time came, I resolved I wouldn't make it any easier for the men who would come for me.

I proceeded to do a set of push-ups and sit-ups and jogged on the spot for what I judged to be at least thirty minutes till I had worked up a fair bit of sweat. I couldn't be sure of the time, because the bastards had taken my watch, but a little bit of sunlight crept in through a crack in the ceiling. It appeared to be late morning.

The old man pointed to his head in the universal gesture to signify someone who was crazy. Maybe he did think I was insane, but he didn't know what I knew, what every soldier knew. When in combat, grab sleep and food whenever you can, because you never know when the next meal or opportunity to rest will come.

The door opened and two gunmen came in. I thought they had come for me, but they ignored me and herded the four fishermen out. The old man turned to look at me. I saw the look of resignation in his eyes. At that moment, facing men armed with AK-47s and with no weapons, I could do nothing. A few minutes later, I heard four gunshots in quick succession, then silence.

As I sat there, I thought of that friendly, old man and the look in his eyes as he was herded away to his death. I got up and began practising a series of combat exercises, pushing myself till my body ached, trying to burn out the rage within me.

When I finished, I sat down, my eyes closed, trying to control my breathing. Trying to calm down. I had four more deaths to avenge.

All afternoon, I sat studying my surroundings. There wasn't much that I found that could be helpful if I was to make any attempt to escape. There were no windows, only one door, likely with guards outside. To top it all, I had no idea where I was. If I was on some godforsaken island, even if I miraculously managed to escape this cell, I wouldn't be able to swim to anywhere safe. I wondered if the Indian government was looking for me after the bloodbath in Hanoi. I didn't think they would do it out of any love for me, but hoped that the fact that they knew an Indian soldier was held captive and now several more Indians, Krishnan included, had paid with their lives, would spur them into action. The problem was that even if they had drones or satellites scanning the area, they had no idea of which shithole I was in, and by the time they found out, it might be too late for me.

I conjured up notions of hijacking a boat and escaping and chuckled. I had no idea where I was, how to sail a boat and hot-wiring one. Being chased and likely blown up in the middle of shark-infested waters was a pretty convoluted way to die. So I sat there and thought of Zoya and Aman. Of how I'd met Zoya, the confident young woman who had stormed into my life. She had drawn me out, made me open up, made me realize that who I was as a man was much more than the sum total of the titles I had held and the work I had done. She had given me strength; she had given me hope; and she had made me realize that my earlier notions as a young soldier had been wrong. Bravery did not lie in physical acts of courage or not being afraid to die but in coming to peace with the choices you made. Zoya had helped me achieve that peace.

Aman. Holding him for the first time, looking into his big eyes and promising him that Daddy would take care of him, while wondering how I could ever be responsible for another life. Remembering my own father, whom I had lost in a car accident when I had just joined the army. Thinking of all the times I had resented him and fought with him, only to appreciate what he'd done for me when I'd become a father myself. What would Aman think of me when he grew up? Would he remember the good times or the times I'd screwed up as a father?

I paused at that thought. As things stood, there was a good chance Aman would grow up without ever knowing who his father was, other than some photos and stories told by Zoya. Over time, I would become a faded memory. Perhaps Zo would marry someone else. I wouldn't ever begrudge her that. I would want her and Aman to have a good life, a good family. Perhaps the person she'd meet would not be as tainted as I was. No dark secrets of the past, no people coming in the dark to kill us. Maybe Zo would enjoy sleeping next to someone who did not wake up several times a night, tormented by some nightmare of his past or another. Maybe he'd be a well-educated executive, the kind of man Zo deserved. They'd have a nicer house, take nicer vacations, Aman would get the best education, go on and do something with his life.

I knew this line of thinking did no good, but I didn't care. I just sat there and wept for the life I had left behind, one I might never go back to. I wept for Zo and Aman and for not being there for them. Most of all, I wept for the imperfect man I was and the troubles I had visited on my family by being who and what I was.

When the door opened that evening, it was Zhang. He had a grim expression on his face.

'Come. My bosses have asked me to move you to another cell.'

I could tell that was not the fate he had in mind for me. I wasn't sure what his bosses had in mind, but as long as it didn't involve immediate execution, it was better than what I had thought my fate would be. As I got up, I weighed my chances. Zhang was alone, unarmed. If I had a chance, if not of escaping, then of sending this devil to hell, this was it. He smiled and I had to give the devil his due. He was a murderous bastard, but he had balls.

'Major, my orders are not to kill you and even if I don't like it, I have to follow them. For now, at least. That doesn't mean I can't hurt you.'

I had seen it before in his eyes. In the alley, and then again when he had been interrogating me. Every person has a weakness, and Zhang's was his ego. I had hurt his ego by taking out his men in Afghanistan, then by leaving him bruised and humiliated at my home, and then again in the alley. Part of him was itching to prove that he was a better than me. That was the part that would likely cause him to make a mistake—one I could perhaps take advantage of when the time came.

If he wanted to play, I was game. I got up and without much ado kicked his left leg from under him. As he fell to one knee, I brought my right fist arcing towards his face. He blocked the blow but couldn't stop my left knee from connecting with his chin. He staggered back, and I could see blood coming out of his mouth.

I stood there, watching him calmly as he got up. 'Zhang, you talk too much. Hanging out with pirates has made you forget what it was to once be a soldier.'

He rushed me. This time I had no element of surprise, so I parried his first blow and then we were grappling, looking for an opening, looking for a way to get some leverage. He tried to headbutt me, but I moved my head to one side and managed to grab his collar and tried to throw him over my hip. Zhang had done this dance many times, so it didn't work out as cleanly or as elegantly as you may imagine or how you've seen people being thrown in judo matches or in the movies, but I did kind of get him down on the ground.

One point to me. Except nobody here bothered what the hell the score was. The winner lived and the loser died. That made for a pretty simple scoring system.

Zhang wrapped his legs around my right leg and rolled, bringing me down, and tried to get on top of me. One point to him.

I hammered him in the face with my fist and he returned the favour, rocking my head back. Points shared, I'd say. Though he was bleeding and I wasn't, so I claim moral victory.

Then we were brawling, all pretence of finesse and style gone. The one edge I thought I had was that Zhang was under orders not to kill me. I had no such restrictions. I went for his eyes, and he grabbed my thumb and bent it back powerfully enough for me to howl. I spat in his face, which brought forth a stream of Chinese invectives, to which I added my list of Hindi gutter-speak when he managed to knee me in the balls. Then I bit his ear.

Yes, you got it right. I bit his ear.

When two men like Zhang and I go for each other, the fight isn't anything like what you would imagine. No fancy moves, no posturing. You see, how we fought was how professional soldiers are trained to fight—dirty, and with only one objective: kill the other bastard as early and as fast as you can. Zhang screamed, and if my balls and face were not in so much pain, I thought I would have smiled. That brought the guards in and they went to work on me. A couple of kicks got me to release his ear, though I was satisfied to see it covered in blood. I rolled to one side and then got up to face the guards.

Two young, fit men, wearing clean, pressed olive-coloured uniforms, but without any visible insignia or marks of identification, both looking at the mayhem in the cell. As one came toward me, I spat out what was in my mouth. A little piece of Zhang's ear, a bunch of blood, and a lot of spittle messed up the poor guy's uniform. I thought he actually recoiled in horror at the madman in front of him spitting out blood. Too bad. I reached in and smashed his Adam's apple. Within a second, messy clothes were the least of his worries as he lay dying. His friend, smarter than he was, shouted for help as he brought up his rifle.

Checkmate. I could do many things, but I couldn't dodge AK-47 bullets and he was too far away for me to disarm. By now Zhang was up, grabbing his ear and screaming in Chinese. Whether that abuse was aimed at me or his subordinates, I never did find out. Either way, I didn't give a shit, having bigger worries than his temper. His flunkies were clearly agitated by what had just happened, for a half-dozen screaming Chinamen rushed in and proceeded to grab me. Zhang was staring at me and I laughed at him.

'Your fucking ear's down there somewhere, unless one of your men stepped on it. Maybe you can find the piece if you look hard enough.'

He growled and barked something in Chinese. One of the men punched me in the gut and I bent forward, retching. He landed another punch on my face and I rewarded him by spitting out more blood onto his face. The others then got to work on me. I'd like to say I fought back, but I was bleeding, tired, in pain and outnumbered six to one by young men pissed off at me having killed one of their pals and having embarrassed their boss, which I was sure would end up in some sort of punishment for them.

I assumed the position—body curled in, trying to protect my head and other vital parts—and took the beating as gamely as I could. After a while, it was a relief to just pass out.

I have only sketchy memories of what followed. I remember seeing some bright light, and for a second wondered if I was dead and headed to Heaven. Some part of my bruised mind wondered idly if there would be a place in Heaven for someone like me. I had never been particularly religious, but I had never denied that there could be a power beyond what we understood or could control. When you were a soldier and knew you could die at any minute and often saw friends die when they had so much to live for, you tended to believe, or at least hope, that things happened for a bigger reason. Either that or life was one big, fucked-up mess and whether you lived or died was just down to dumb luck. It was usually easier on one's sanity to believe the former.

Anyway, when my eyes opened, I wasn't in Heaven, unless it stank of stale piss. That was my first memory when I woke up. Someone was trying to take off my clothes and scrub me clean with cold water. I tried resisting, but hardly had the strength and passed out again. When I next awoke, it was on a cot, with bandages around my midriff, my head, and my left hand. As I opened my eyes and looked at myself and felt the bandages, I figured I must look like a Mummy in some bad horror movie. My kind of movie, and most definitely not something I could ever convince Zoya to watch. That brought a smile to my face, and I realized that even smiling hurt. Someone forced some water into my mouth, and I passed out again.

Then I slept. I remember that because unlike the previous occasions, I dreamt a lot. I don't remember all of the dreams, but I do remember two. In one, I saw my father and mother on the road. Just like that. They were walking, talking to each other, holding hands. They looked no older than when they had passed away. I accosted them, asking them why they had left me and never called. I distinctly remember giving them my phone number and pleading with them to at least call even if they didn't want to meet me. I told them my number was encrypted so they didn't have to worry about anyone tapping their calls. They asked for my number again, as if they couldn't hear me clearly, and I kept trying to tell them, but they didn't get it. I felt my chest constrict as they faded away and I kept shouting out to them.

In the second dream, I had a little crystal or perhaps a piece of a statue in my hand. There were people around me, looking for another like it. I don't remember all the specifics, but I remember the feeling that Zo and Aman were there. I climbed down into some dark tunnel, where it was really dirty and dangerous, and found the other piece, and when I put the two together, everything lit up in a warm glow. I woke feeling more at peace than I ever had.

What the hell did it all mean? I'm no shrink, but the missing piece that needed to be completed was perhaps me, and I needed to discover the complete me to really bring happiness to myself and to Zo and Aman. But what was the complete me? Maybe I was just reading too much into what were nothing more than meaningless dreams conjured up by my damaged and bruised brain.

'Good morning, young man. You certainly slept a lot, though you needed it after what they did to you.'

I turned my head towards the voice. It came from an Indian man, perhaps a few years older than me.

He was wearing a faded shirt and torn jeans. His hair was overgrown, and his beard had the unkempt look of someone who had grown a beard not to make any sort of fashion statement, but simply because he had not had the opportunity to shave. His body was thin, but his broad shoulders indicated he had lost weight due to lack of food more than any desire to lose weight or stay fit. He was staring at my back when I turned to try to get up.

'Keep lying down.'

Given how much it hurt to try to move, that was advice I was perfectly happy to take. 'Who are you?'

By way of reply, he rolled up his right sleeve up to his shoulder. There I saw a tattoo that I had on my own back, the same one the man had drawn with his own blood in the note I had seen.

He smiled as I said his code name out aloud. 'Invictus.'

For all the pain I was in, I smiled back. I might or might not live much longer, but I had achieved part of my mission.

Despite the pain I was in, knowing that I had finally met the man whom I had set out to locate made me sit up straight. 'Partner, your note got out to the right people. They know you're being held. They care enough to try to get you out.'

I would have hoped he would have reacted with more enthusiasm. After all, wasn't the whole point of his writing the note to try to get word back to the Indian government that he was alive and that he was a Chinese prisoner?

He got up and began pacing around the cell, and, to my confusion, began to chuckle. 'I have no idea who you are, but you're incredibly naïve if you think there is any hope of me getting out of here. Now that you're here as well, I'd say you're as screwed as I am.'

When I asked him what he meant, he laughed out loud.

'What's so funny?'

He must have sensed the anger and outrage in my voice,

so he held out his palms in a conciliatory gesture. 'Nothing personal. Nothing personal at all. I saw the tattoo on your back, so I suppose you are or were part of the same family I used to belong to. It's just that you have just become part of a long list of soldiers, who become pawns in the games spies play and get screwed over.'

I couldn't help but agree, but I wondered what specifically he had in mind and why he wasn't happier that the Indian government still cared to try to get him out. Of course, I didn't say that quite as eloquently. What I said was, 'You're a pretty ungrateful bastard. Do you know how many people have died because of your bloody note?'

He held out his hand and pulled me up to a sitting position. 'No point arguing on an empty stomach. The guards left our gruel for the evening while you were sleeping. Let's chat while we eat.'

The porridge was terrible, but I wolfed it down as he asked me to introduce myself. Then he began with his tale.

'My name is Srini Naladala. I was a major in the Paras, just like you, only I left the army perhaps when you were just finishing up your own training. I joined the Special Frontier Force, did some covert ops near the China border, and that must have got the attention of some people higher up, because soon enough I was offered a job in R&AW. Nice promotion, perks and since I didn't have a family, I didn't mind the extra money that came with every job that took me to some other godforsaken hellhole.'

I'd heard such stories before, and to be honest, I was in a similar spot, even though I had not been formally hired into the Indian intelligence apparatus. However, that was where Srini's story began to take an unexpected turn.

'I did a bunch of work in Afghanistan and Pakistan. A bunch of jihadis—Taliban, ISIS, and a bunch of freelance loonies, all worked over and bombed to hell by the Americans—were looking for new pastures, and were being pushed into Kashmir by the ISI. I'm sure you encountered many of those fine specimens during your time in Kashmir.'

I had to smile in reply as he continued. 'My job wasn't to kill them. It was to redirect them.'

'What?'

He chuckled, though there was no humour in his voice. 'That's the kind of fancy word the spooks use when they make missions seem simpler than they are; missions where they can continue to sit in their conference rooms and present slides while fools like us put our necks on the line.'

The bitterness he felt was palpable, and perhaps understandable, because I knew when a man like him was caught by the enemy, the government would typically deny any relationship with him. Plausible deniability, another fancy phrase used by men in suits who put people like us in harm's way without wanting to get any blood on their neatly pressed suits.

'My job was to get the jihadis all worked up about what the Chinese were doing to Muslims in Xinjiang. The reality is bad enough—millions in concentration camps, a systematic programme to wipe out traditional Islamic beliefs and a total clampdown on any dissent. Many jihadis were easy to convince that they should fight that enemy instead of coming to India. Some old-timers among the Afghans had fought the Soviets, and saw this as another crusade against yet another godless Communist regime. It was hard to penetrate China, but there were some people in place, and the ball was slowly rolling. A few small attacks had taken place, but the spooks wanted more, wanted the hardcore ISIS- and Al Qaeda-trained fighters coming to India to go over to China instead.'

He took a sip of water and continued. 'To do that meant going even deeper into jihadi circles and that's when I stumbled upon Project Lotus.'

The name sent a chill through me. I told Srini what I knew of Lotus and how I myself had been mixed up in the chaos that it had unleashed. When I finished, his eyes widened.

'I'm surprised you're still alive, Major. Either you are very lucky or you do indeed have friends in the right places looking out for you.'

'What do you mean?'

'Lots of Indian officers were involved along with Pakistanis in Lotus at the start. This all started as just a drug-smuggling ring, but somewhere along the way the Chinese came in and made it something else altogether. For the Chinese, the drugs were just a fringe benefit. Allowed them to arm some jihadis who they could get to do their bidding. The real benefit they saw was something else altogether.'

Now I was confused. I got the drug-smuggling part, but something that hadn't made sense to me was why elite

Chinese troops would be involved. When I asked Srini that, he smiled.

'Major, I did not send out that note with any hope of getting rescued. I've been in Chinese custody for over eighteen months. At first, they were pretty rough on me, and I told them what they wanted to know after holding out for as long as I could. The Chinese never really sweated me for anything more than what I had figured out about Project Lotus. They were keen to know everything I did about it and what I had passed on to my bosses.'

Something wasn't adding up for me. 'Srini, Gopal and the PM were genuinely surprised to see that you were alive. They really wanted to help you get out. The Chinese never let our government know they had you. If they had no real use for you, why didn't they just kill you and make you disappear? Why keep you alive for so long?'

He looked at me and sighed loudly. 'Zhang told me that they had decided to execute me. That was a year or so ago. Then something changed.'

'What?'

He leaned towards me. 'Zhang seemed very pissed off. Now that I think of the timing, it must have been right after your run-in with him in Afghanistan. These guys have moles all over the place—in the US and in India. And I'm not talking about small fry. I think they have people on their payroll in senior places, people well above our pay grades. After Afghanistan, Zhang beat me up pretty badly, and wanted to know about an op I had begun to infiltrate but hadn't told them anything about. I had told them everything about Lotus. Everybody breaks under torture, so I had to give them something, but I had held back on the other operation. Now Zhang wanted to know everything I knew. He seemed paranoid that this not get compromised like Lotus had. He tortured me, beat me, and then after a few months of not being able to take it anymore, I told him what I knew.'

I could see his head drop in shame. For any soldier, it was hard to admit that they had given in, that they had surrendered to the enemy. But I knew from long experience that it is only in the movies that the stoic and tough hero holds out in the face of torture. The reality of torture is not what they show you in films. Fingernails are pulled out, teeth are broken, bones are smashed, electric shocks are applied to the genitals—and that's just the basics for someone who really is serious about torturing you. In our training, we had been told time and again that if we were ever captured by the enemy, our first recourse would be to escape, because there was no way we could hold out in the face of sustained torture. I held his shoulder.

'No shame, brother. You did what any of us would have done. Even the best of us.'

When he looked up at me, there was a look of defiance. 'Major, my body broke, but my spirit didn't. I gave up hope of making it out alive, but I saw the diary where Zhang was making notes of my interrogation. Back then, seeing how compliant I seemed to have become, they started allowing me to take short walks outside my cell. One day, I heard them talking about an Indian crew they had brought in for ransom, and I overheard the Indians in the cell next to me. One day when they took me out for a walk, I knocked out my guard and broke into Zhang's office. They thought

I was trying to escape. They beat me to an inch of my life and never allowed me outside the cell again. But I managed to get a piece of paper from his diary—a paper with the operation name and some Chinese words on it. I used my blood to write a message and passed it on the Indians in the next cell. The rest you know. It wasn't a plea to be rescued, Major. It was an attempt to warn folks back in Delhi about this operation.'

'What operation is this?'

'Camel.'

With all that had happened in the previous few days, I had not had the time to connect the dots, but when Naladala said the word, it all came back. That was the word Gopal's spooks had decrypted, and that was the word Karzai had told me was the title of the hard disk in his possession.

What was Operation Camel and why was it so important that the Chinese were willing to take such risks to keep it a secret?

'Tell me what you know.'

When Naladala finished, my head was spinning. Gopal and his crew had the note, far away in Delhi. Karzai had the hard disk, and he was likely dead, and I was in this cell, unable to do anything about the information I now had.

The door to the cell opened and four guards came in, holding rifles at the ready.

'You, come with us.'

As I was marched out, I figured that I was about to get the answers to my questions.

I was marched into a conference room, which looked like it would have been more at home in some swanky corporate office than in a prison where pirates brought their prey or where the likes of Zhang got off on torturing their prisoners. Sitting at the table was Zhang, his ear heavily bandaged, and a short, slim woman.

She looked Chinese, but her hair was dyed blonde and she was dressed in a sharp business suit, looking totally out of place. They must have paid Chinese spies well because her suit seemed to have come straight off some mannequin in a luxury boutique—one of those fancy European-sounding brands which, truth be told, I would never be able to afford and would struggle to pronounce. Her hair was tied in a bun and her high heels clicked on the floor as she walked up to me. I could smell perfume in the air as she came closer and then she stopped, looking at me, a slight smile forming on the edges of her mouth. She fired off a long sentence in Chinese to which Zhang replied with a monosyllabic grunt. The woman chuckled and Zhang coloured.

I took a step forward. 'Is she asking if I'm the one who tweaked your ear, Zhang?'

His face contorted in rage and he took a step towards me, but the woman barked an order in Chinese and Zhang stopped. It was very clear who the boss here was. The woman looked at me and spoke, this time in slightly accented, but otherwise flawless, English. 'You are quite a troublemaker.'

That wasn't the first time I had been accused of that, and I really had nothing to say in return, so I stayed silent as the woman continued. 'We would have preferred to have solved your problem in Mumbai itself, but given the circumstances, I am happy you are here. I was curious as to who this fabled Major Ghosh is who had caused us so much trouble over the last couple of years.'

I had been called many things, but never fabled, which I supposed was a step up from being called a troublemaker.

'Now, please tell me all that you know about Camel. We know the note reached the Indian government and they decrypted the fact that it has something to do with Camel. We put you in the same cell as your fellow prisoner because we wanted you to compare notes. We will interrogate him separately and see if we spot anything you told him that you withheld from us. We can make this as simple or as complicated as you wish, but know that our patience is undoubtedly more than your threshold for pain.'

There were warning bells going off all over my head. How the hell did she know the Indians had decrypted the word 'Camel'? I had not said that to Naladala. That meant that they had a mole pretty deep and pretty high in the Indian establishment. Also, I worried for Naladala. Relieved at having found him, I had told him a lot about my role in dismantling Lotus. I had been careful to leave out any mention of Karzai or details of the current operation and the plans Gopal had made. Unfortunately, the Chinese would likely believe I had told him more than I had and would torture him to extract that information from him.

'Staying silent is not a sustainable solution, Major. I

would highly encourage you to start speaking unless you want us to practise more unpleasant forms of persuasion. We are good at that, you know.'

I had no smart ideas, so I looked at Zhang. 'Is this lady your boss? She speaks like a typical bureaucrat and could bore us to death. Is that the plan?'

This time the woman flushed, and I thought I saw a hint of a grin on Zhang's face.

Zhang's boss looked at me, her eyes hard, all humour gone. 'I can see why so many people seem to want to kill you, Major. It is well deserved.'

Touché. That wasn't such a bad retort.

'I gathered from your chat with the prisoner that you really don't know why we have you here.'

I cursed myself. Of course, they would have the cell bugged. Like an idiot I had babbled on with Srini about what I knew.

'Major, we do not have much time. Even if I assume what you told my gullible subordinate about having a tracer in your bloodstream is another of your fantastic lies, we want to leave soon. So talk.'

Zhang coloured again at the insult. Clearly this boss-subordinate relationship had seen better days. Part of my training wasn't just in blowing stuff up and killing people in inventive ways. An important part of any special forces training programme is to learn to look for leverage—in simple words, anything that can be used to your tactical advantage. No doubt Zhang had got similar training in the Chinese army, but his boss seemed to have spent more of her time in conference rooms than in the field.

'Zhang, why are you so gullible, man? Be savvier like your boss here. Maybe you'll get a raise and be able to afford fancy suits like her.'

His boss just shook her head. 'Get on with it.'

The woman nodded to one of the guards behind me and he slammed the butt of his rifle into the small of my back, sending me stumbling forward as another guard kicked me, sending me to my knees. I could feel the barrel of a rifle at my neck as the woman leaned down over me.

'You do not refer to me as 'the lady' or 'the boss'. My name is Comrade Chen Lao. I am a director in the MSS and normally I would not bother overseeing the interrogation of a low-level capture like you. In your case, I have to say the pleasure will be all mine.'

Zhang was smiling, and I realized I was in a spot, and for once, had no real plan. The Indian military was not going to swoop in to rescue me. I had no real bargaining chips to keep myself alive, and the one man who actually had something of value to Chen and company, Karzai, was dead. He was also the one man who could have helped me, but that was hard to do when you were lying dead on a roof of a Hanoi market. The Indians hadn't made me swallow any fancy tracking solution, but Karzai had, something that would allow him to track me for up to forty-eight hours and then dissolve in my bloodstream. Of course, that would have meant something if Karzai hadn't been dead.

Out of options, out of hope, there was nothing I could do but stall for time and create as much of a nuisance of myself as I could before they killed me.

Oh, that much I had reconciled to by now. There was no way they would let me go alive, and I realized my earlier bullshit story about the Indians tracking me had only served to accelerate my death as they clearly looked to be in a hurry to wrap things up.

Zhang slapped me hard. 'We don't have all day, Major.'

'You seem to be in a hurry. Did this bitch promise you a good time later in the evening?'

I thought he split my lip with his next blow. 'You will learn some manners, Major. We will leave soon and also want some time with your friend, so I have just under an hour with you.'

I was about to say something when he hit me again, with two guards holding down my hands and another grabbing my neck. 'I am going to enjoy this hour, Major. My orders are to get the information I need from you, and if I cannot, then to kill you before we leave.'

'I have no idea what you want, Zhang. We can save you the time and the pain. I have no idea what you want.'

'That's too bad, Major. Because I plan to take every single second I have. I'm in no hurry. No hurry at all.'

Chen barked out her question at me. 'What have the Indians found out about Operation Camel?'

The truthful answer was that the government had no idea what Camel was other than the one word they had decrypted. However, saying that would just lead them to put a bullet in my head faster. So I blundered on, weaving what

I had learned from Naladala with pure fiction, hoping to unnerve and unbalance my enemies and perhaps buy myself some time, though for what I had no idea.

'You think you're really smart, don't you? Must be all that Sun Tzu bullshit you peddle.'

That earned me another slap from Zhang.

I spat out blood and continued. 'Lotus was a great op. Earned dollars to pay for jihadis to wreak mayhem against the US in Afghanistan and against India in Kashmir. Weakens both, with the fringe benefit of weakening their societies by feeding the drug problem, especially in the US. Smart, very smart. If one were to get all philosophical about it, one might say it is poetic justice—a sort of convoluted payback in kind for the Opium Wars the West inflicted on you long ago.'

Chen's eyebrows arched high. Maybe she had not expected that of me.

I smiled at her. 'Just because I don't wear a fucking Gucci suit doesn't mean I can't think or know history. We're taught strategy in addition to beating the shit out of enemies like you, and at a strategic level I can appreciate it. Also, minimal risk to the MSS. As they say, you were willing to fight hard—fight right down to the last Pakistani! Enough deluded generals and jihadis there to do your dirty work, for money or for promises of virgins in the afterlife.'

Chen nudged Zhang aside. 'I am impressed, Major. That is the clearest articulation of Lotus that I have heard yet. Unfortunately, we know the op was compromised and we lost most of our assets. So having an intellectual discussion about it will not help prolong your life. Tell us what the Indians know about Camel.'

'Look, I know I hold very few cards and I am not a glutton for punishment, so I'll tell you what you want to know. Just give Naladala an easy death. He's been through enough and really knows nothing more than what he's already told you. Pretty smart again—pivot from what Lotus was doing to actively redirect the jihadis against the Indians in Kashmir as well as foment another coup in Pakistan to put a friendly general in the saddle. You've been missing a lapdog in Islamabad ever since Karimi's head was taken. So you decided to funnel your dirty money to not just any terror attacks in India, but ones specially targeted at security forces to provoke a military reaction against Pakistan. Create a sense of crisis and lack of belief in the new civilian government there, and in parallel get your man in the seat in Islamabad to escalate the conflict against India. New Delhi gets weakened by fighting Pakistan, and once again, no real risk to you folks—the Pakistanis do all the fighting and dying. Far better for you to let the Pakistanis weaken India than to have to get into a fight with us.'

'Nothing new there for me, Major. I know Naladala told you the basics and the rest anyone with even your minimal level of intelligence can figure out. Regurgitating that won't prolong your life. What is it that the Indians know?'

This was where I had to bullshit convincingly. 'They know it all. They got their hands on an encrypted hard drive that had all the goodies on Camel. They know the names of the Pakistani generals involved in the coup attempt and know your specific plans for terror strikes in India. As we speak, they could be warning the government in Pakistan and launching strikes against the terror cells.'

I didn't know how good a spy Chen was, but she must have been a good poker player because I got no reaction out of her. Zhang on the other hand must have been a better soldier than a poker player, because his eyes darted towards her.

The reality was that for all her posturing, Chen was hardly on top of the totem pole. An operation of the sort that Camel seemed to be couldn't have been run only by her. It must have the backing of people far above her pay grade. Another thing common to bureaucrats all over the world—they hate looking bad in front of their bosses. So, poker face or not, I could almost imagine the panic in Chen's mind as she thought of the plan going bust and her bosses blaming her for it. I suspected that in the world she operated in, failure did not mean a lower bonus or a pink slip, but perhaps a stint in a concentration camp or a bullet in the head.

She pulled Zhang aside. There was a lot of furious whispering back and forth. Without further ado, they stormed out of the room.

Seemed like I had bought myself a bit more time, but to what end? No matter how this turned out, it looked like the only outcome was for me to end up dead.

The next fifteen minutes were frenetic and painful. First, Naladala was bundled into the room by three guards and Zhang went to work on him. The poor man knew nothing of what I had told the Chinese and earned a bit of an extra beating at first, but soon it was apparent to Zhang that Naladala was being truthful when he said he knew nothing of what the Indian government was up to, as I had not mentioned any of it to him.

Bloodied and bruised, he was led out of the room. As he left the room, he looked at me and shouted. 'Where is the cavalry you promised?'

I sat there, feeling terrible. I had told him what I had told Zhang and gang—that the Indian government would be tracking me and would come for us. I knew no such thing was going to happen. All I was doing was buying some time.

Chen exited the room, leaving me with Zhang and his four men. He was glaring at me. 'You do realize, Major, that no matter what happens, you are a dead man.'

I spat at him. 'You have such a firm grasp of the fucking obvious, don't you?'

He slapped me and this time I began to sing, one of those Badshah numbers you hear on the radio all the time—catchy with virtually indecipherable lyrics. I didn't think Zhang's taste in music ran to the singer, and the Punjabi words must have really messed with his mind. So, he did what he seemed to do whenever he was at a loss. He slapped me again, which caused me to unload on him with the choicest of Punjabi abuses—telling him to do all kinds of inventive things in bed, starting with his female relatives and then progressing on to goats and camels.

'What the hell are you talking about?'

I stopped my rant and looked him the eye, trying to be as serious as I could. 'Those were the code names the Indians have for their counter-intel operations put in place to defeat Camel. You are so royally fucked. When your plans go for a toss, I suspect your bosses will not even bother reprimanding you. I see a fortune cookie for you saying that you have earned a bullet in the head for all your fuckups.'

Which of course meant he hit me again.

I thought he had broken my nose because it hurt like hell, and I wondered whether a broken nose would leave me with a rakish look Zo would appreciate or just make me look like even more of an ogre. Then I reminded myself that the chances of Zo seeing me ever again were close to zero. I was going to die in this bloody prison; nobody would likely know what had happened to me, and if Camel was what it seemed to be, many, many more people would die.

Zhang leaned over me. 'Why are you so difficult?'

I looked at him and stuck my tongue out at him, which earned me another blow.

'Are you a fucking retard, Zhang? I've told you everything I know. I can't do anything more. Either kill me or let me go, because your plans are going to soon go belly up. The Indians know all about Camel, and you are so screwed. You and your fancy-pants boss just don't get it, do you? Who knows, as you sit there messing with my face, Indian Mirages may be taking out some damn terror camps, and this time the Pakistani civilian government may well be thanking India for doing it. They in turn might be arresting some of your lapdog generals.'

The door opened and I heard a familiar voice. 'Major, you are a good bullshitter, but not as good as you think. The Indians know nothing of Camel.'

I looked up at the door and for once I was so shocked that I shut up, not knowing what to say.

The man standing there was Sandeep Krishnan.

'Good evening, Major. I see you haven't lost your talent for creating trouble.'

I said nothing as Krishnan kept speaking, still trying to come to grips with the fact that he was there in front of me, gradually surmising the only reason he could be with Zhang and the Chinese.

'Why, Major, is that just anger or righteous indignation I see in your eyes?'

I am a simple soldier, and just on principle, I would have

shot someone for using the words 'righteous indignation' in the middle of a conversation. I mean, who does that? Add to that the fact that the one saying those words was a corrupt, traitorous bastard like Krishnan. It made killing him a no-brainer. Of course, being held down by four men and with a rifle pointed at my back meant my dreams of lashing out at him remained precisely that and nothing more.

Krishnan was now joined by Chen. He turned to look at her with a deference that made it clear who the boss was. 'He has been making all this stuff up. I confirmed the Indians don't have any more information about Camel other than finding out the name from the note. They are trying to decrypt it but can't with just what they have. Also, he's not being tracked by them. That is another of his stories. I checked back with Delhi specifically on whether they had any trackers on him and they said no. So just shoot him and get it over with already.'

Zhang chipped in with his own opinion, which no doubt was not biased at all by how much of a pain in the ass I had been for him. 'Comrade, I agree. Let us shoot him. I'll do it right now.'

I blew him a kiss. 'I love you too, sweetheart.'

That earned me a scowl. Don't you hate enemy assassins who don't have a sense of humour?

Chen was looking at me with a smile on her face.

'Something funny, Comrade Chen?'

She began laughing. 'You are entertaining, Major. I do admire your courage, but as they say, you are now at the end of the road.'

'Zhang, I get. Fucked in the head from too many falls as a kid. Can't get any other job and gets drafted into the army. Realizes he gets off on hurting people and becomes a commando, then a gun for hire. Still wants to prove he's good at what he does. You, lady in the suit with the nice perfume, I'm guessing you're some bigshot in Beijing. I get you, trying to do your job, but hating that the idiot of a subordinate you have in Zhang screwed things up so bad that you have to step out of your air-conditioned conference room and get your hands dirty.'

I wasn't looking at her, but at Krishnan. It was one thing to fight and kill an enemy who was acting on their own orders, doing what they thought to be right. It was quite another to be confronted with a traitor, someone who had turned on those who counted on him. I knew I wasn't getting out alive, but before I died, I crystallized my last mission as a simple one—somehow, I would kill this traitor.

'But you, Krishnan, I don't get. What made you turn traitor? Was it just money or did they have videos of you with Vietnamese boys?'

Krishnan slapped me, though I could tell by his grimace that he hurt himself more than he hurt me. 'I wish they had just shot you. I told you I didn't steal my government's money, and I didn't. I just found a better paymaster.'

I wanted to smash his face in as he said that with such nonchalance. I realized that Anita must have reached out to him—she had mentioned reaching out to an embassy officer. This bastard was the direct cause of her death. I also realized I was fast running out of things to say to stall things, so I decided to move up things up a notch. Escape be damned. I would settle for buying enough time to get an opportunity to kill the traitor in front of me.

'You think you know it all, Krishnan. You must have told Chen what a bigshot you are, not the reality that you're just another bureaucrat who only knows what your bosses allow you to know. I sat in on the planning with Gopal and the prime minister himself. And it's not just the note Naladala got out. They have figured out how to use it along with the hard disk on Camel I got out of Korengal and passed onto the government. Bet you didn't know that.'

Krishnan hit me again, but I was looking at Chen. I could see the indecision in her eyes. 'Comrade Chen, you never asked me about the disk. Because you have no idea where it is. I bet you haven't even told your bosses it's missing. Maybe you were hoping it was destroyed.'

'Where is the hard disk? Tell us where it is.'

When I said nothing, Zhang hit my broken nose again and I screamed in agony. I was out of ideas, mad as hell and didn't feel like just sitting there and getting hit. So I quickly decided on what to do and executed my plan.

My plan being falling face first on the table and shaking uncontrollably.

'What the fuck is happening to him? Is he having a seizure?' the traitor said.

Krishnan had given me a good idea. So I began to spit out saliva and bang my head on the table. I had never been good at acting. In school, my dramatics career had been limited to a single role, that of a tree, where all I was expected to do was stand and swing my arms gently like branches. I didn't think my drama teacher had trusted me to do anything more complicated. I wished he could see me now, playing the role of my life as I interspersed my flopping around on the table and drooling with random abuses in Bengali. Why Bengali? Why the fuck not? Just thought it would add to the drama.

Zhang's boss cried out, her voice almost a high-pitched shriek. 'Get the doctor! We can't lose him before we know where the disk is!'

Two guards let go of my shoulders and left the room as I kept flopping around. The odds were still terrible, and I was still going to die, but that was as good an opportunity as I was going to get.

As the two remaining guards tried to grab me, I snapped my head back, breaking one of their noses. The other loosened his grip in panic and I bit him hard and he screamed. The one or two seconds it took for people to figure out that I wasn't really having a seizure was enough for me to jump across the table and grab the pen I had seen lying on the table in front of Krishnan. He was looking at me, his eyes wide in shock as I grabbed the back of his head with my left hand and used my right hand to stab him through his right eye with the pen.

Righteous indignation, my ass!

It is debatable whether a pen is mightier than a sword, but it sure is mightier than the human eyeball and brain. Krishnan was dead within seconds and I turned towards the guards, holding his body in front of me. As they unloaded on me with their rifles, I threw Krishnan's body in front of me and dove under the table.

So this was how it all ended. Not a bad way to go, I guessed. I felt a pang of regret at not being able to see Zoya and Aman again. I had done all I could. I saw the guards scramble under the table and saw the barrel of the first rifle pointing at me.

Game over.

That was when I heard a series of whooshing sounds followed by explosions that shook everything around me, bouncing me off the ground so hard I hit my head against the underside of the table. There was silence in the room for a second and then I heard another set of explosions and pieces of the ceiling came tumbling down around me. The gun barrel had disappeared. Then I heard frantic shouts as people left the room to deal with what had just hit them.

One of the guards was on the floor with pieces of the ceiling all over him. The other one was scrambling around on the ground for his rifle when I stepped over to him and kicked him hard in the neck. He went down and didn't get up. I picked up his rifle and left the room.

I had no idea what had happened, but all I knew was that, out of nowhere, I had a chance. I couldn't see Zhang or Chen anywhere and the door was wide open. I ran out into the corridor, working my way back to the direction of the cell where Naladala and I had been kept. A single guard was standing near the cell, disoriented and panicked. When I nearly ran into him, he looked up at me as if seeking instructions instead of confronting me with the rifle he held in his hands. My elbow came up in a wide arc and made solid contact with the side of his jaw and he went down. I stomped him on the neck, once, twice, and he didn't get up. He was one of the bastards who had pummelled me, and I wasn't feeling particularly humanitarian. The cell was locked from the outside and I shot the lock and kicked the door open.

Naladala was in a corner of the cell, looking at me with eyes as wide as saucers. 'What's going on?'

'Damned if I know, but let's get out of here.'

I tossed him the rifle I was carrying and picked up the dead guard's rifle outside.

'Still good with a gun, Major?'

He grinned at me. 'I always thought I'd die in that damned cell, executed with a bullet to the back of the head. At least now I have a chance to die fighting.'

Yup, he was a Para, all right.

We went down the corridor, covering each other, but at first there were no signs of any enemies. Naladala was weakened and bloodied and I had a broken nose and perhaps a couple of cracked ribs, but when the first guards showed up in front of us, we both reacted with the instinct that came with years of training. I knelt and put a round in the first man, while Naladala took out the second man with a three-round burst.

'Major, I know the way to Zhang's office. There was an exit near it. Follow me.'

With those words, he ran to the right, me a few steps

behind. There had been no more explosions, but I could hear scattered gunfire outside. I wondered if the explosions had been some sort of accident, but now it seemed like this camp was under attack. From whom and to what end was not clear, but I was happy enough to be still alive, and with a rifle in my hands. I saw the door ahead and tapped Naladala on the shoulder.

'Slow down. There's firing outside and perhaps multiple tangos around. Let me go first and see if the coast is clear.'

The first thing I saw when I opened the door was clear skies and trees all around me, soft sand under my feet, and pristine, blue water visible in the distance through the tree line. This could have been a bloody beach resort if it hadn't been occupied by Zhang and his thugs, who doled out hospitality of a far more brutal variety than the Taj. I swept left and right to see if anyone was around and while I heard a single shot in the distance, the coast seemed to be clear. I had no idea of how we would get away but being in the open at least meant we had more of a fighting chance than being cooped up indoors.

I signalled Naladala to follow me and crept towards the right. While it was tempting to make straight for the water, being caught in the open gap between the trees was likely to get us killed faster versus working our way to the beach through the cover the thicker foliage on the right would provide.

I turned the corner and came face to face with Zhang, who was holding a pistol in his hand. I thought he was as shocked as I was, but just as I saw him, I heard the sound of a helicopter taking off just ahead of me. That distraction cost me a split second of reaction time. That time was all someone with the kind of training Zhang needed.

Then he did what he and Krishnan had been advocating all along. He shot me.

Don't listen to any idiot who tries to convince you that if you've been shot once, it makes the next time any easier to bear. I've been shot many times, and every single time it hurt like hell. This was no exception.

I fell back against the wall, shouting and swearing. I had moved to the side just in time to avoid being shot in the gut. Or I give myself too much credit. Zhang had not really been expecting to see me and had fired on reflex. If he had taken a second more to aim and fire, I'm sure I would be dead. I'm not complaining, because whatever the reason, the good news was that I was still alive. The bad news was that the bullet had hit my left hand just below the elbow and, judging by the searing pain and the weird angle at which my hand seemed to be hanging, he had broken it.

Zhang seemed pleased enough with his handiwork. I suspected the fucker was happy I wasn't dead so he could kill me up close and personal and enjoy it. He took out a knife from his belt and came closer, a smile on his face.

Being unarmed, no pun intended about my broken left arm, and facing a man armed with a gun and a knife wasn't great odds.

Zhang probably realized that and seemed to be taking his time. 'Any last requests, Major?'

'Yeah, could I have some Gobi Manchurian?' he glared at me as I finished my request. 'With some Hakka noodles and a nice cold Kingfisher on the side.'

I'd once again done one of the few things I do consistently well—piss people off. He shouted and launched himself at me, his knife arcing out at me in a blow that was aimed straight at my heart. What does an unarmed man with a ruined left arm do at a time like that?

Why, lift the ruined arm and use it as a shield, of course. My arm was already broken and hurt like hell, so why not mess it up some more to try and save my life? The knife entered the fleshy portion just above my elbow and I swear I actually cried when the tip of the knife emerged from the other side of my arm. Zhang couldn't believe I had just done what I'd done, otherwise he would probably have just shot me with the pistol he still had in his left hand. I didn't wait for him to do so. I slammed my head into his face and was gratified to hear his nose crunch. He raised both hands to his wrecked nose, quite conveniently for me, as it left his body wide open. It was too tempting an opportunity to pass up, and I brought my right knee up into his groin.

Zhang bent forward, dropping his gun. Perhaps wondering which agony was worse—the one he felt in his nose or further down where my knee had perhaps seriously impaired his ability to ever produce little baby Zhangs. I thought I would tilt the balance in favour of the nose by scything my right elbow up at a forty-five-degree angle, making solid contact with his already broken nose. That must have hurt because he screamed all kinds of incomprehensible shit in Chinese and staggered back.

Naladala had appeared on the scene by now, raising his rifle, but hesitating, perhaps taking in the bizarre scene before him. Me, standing there with a knife sticking out of my arm, and Zhang standing there, blood all over his shirt and screaming in Chinese.

If Zhang had not killed Anita or Randhawa, or come for my family, or stabbed Ravi, or been the cause of Karzai's death, I might have left him there, unconscious but alive, and figured out how to escape. Unfortunately for Zhang, he had done all of those, so when he looked up at me and saw the look in my eyes, he knew what was coming. To give credit where it was due, he didn't beg for mercy. Instead, he looked down, trying to pick up his gun. Maybe he still fancied his chances against a guy with a broken hand, a knife sticking out of his arm and no visible weapons. He was right on the first two counts, but wrong on the third. I had a weapon. My pal Zhang had gifted it to me, in a manner of speaking. As Zhang reached for his gun, I pulled the knife out of my arm.

It hurt like hell, and I let go a stream of Hindi abuses which I hoped compared favourably with the abuses Zhang had unloaded when I had broken his nose. Even if I didn't win the contest of whose vocabulary of swear words was better, I won the contest that mattered more—who walked away alive. I took a step towards Zhang and, even as he brought the gun up, stabbed him in the neck.

As Zhang died, we could hear the helicopter's noise receding. Someone had got away, and my instinct told me Comrade Chen had made her way to whatever definition of safety awaited a Chinese spy who had fucked up an operation as badly as she had. Whatever it was, she had clearly judged it to be better than hanging around here. At any rate, she had demonstrated the instinct common to bureaucrats and politicians the world over—bail out at the first sign of trouble and leave the soldiers to do the fighting and dying in your place.

I could see two pillars of smoke in the distance and hear occasional gunfire. Whoever had attacked this place was not done yet.

'What the hell is going on?'

I had no more of an idea than Naladala did, but whatever it was, it offered us our best opportunity of getting away. My arm was broken but I had no desire to lose it forever, so I took the time to make a sling out of Zhang's shirt and took his pistol and set out towards the tree line. Naladala a step behind. We had gone perhaps only a few metres when six men appeared in front of us.

Men carrying AK-47s. Men wearing black. Men in masks. Zhang's men.

They froze when they saw us. Whatever had happened out here, they had been under attack. Who knows, maybe they were coming back to report to Zhang? Or even coming back to regroup, or retreating to their base? Whatever they were planning, they had not expected to see the two of us, out in the open, with the corpse of their commander lying behind us.

For a second, it was almost comical the way we stared at each other—them trying to process what they saw and decide how to react, us trying to think of how we'd get out of this alive. Naladala brought that stand-off to an end by spraying his rifle on full auto at the men. At a range of fifty metres, weakened by his long imprisonment, and totally out of practice, Naladala didn't hit anyone. I suspected most of his shots went high, but the men scattered, diving for cover. As did we. I saw a large boulder to our right, and we scrambled behind it just as the Chinese recovered and bullets began pinging off the rock.

'What now, Major?'

I could see the hope in Naladala's eyes. He had reckoned he would die in a Chinese cell. Now he was free and outside, no longer alone, and with a rifle in his hands. It was natural that he had begun to get his hopes up, to think he could be free again, go home again, wherever home was.

Unfortunately, I wasn't in a position to offer him much hope. 'Got any ammo left?'

He shook his head.

'All I have is this pistol. Zhang fired one shot at me, and I have no idea how many he may have fired previously with whatever chaos was taking place out here. I can see one bullet in the chamber. So I have between one and eight rounds.'

Between one and eight rounds for the pistol. Wielded by a guy who had a broken arm, supported by a man with a rifle and no bullets. Against six men with AK-47s. None of whom had been shot, stabbed in the arm, tortured, or imprisoned for an extended period and who were no doubt seriously pissed off at all the chaos that had suddenly hit their cosy little compound.

In other words, we were well and truly fucked.

Naladala saw the answer in my eyes before I said anything. 'That bad?'

'Looks like it.'

'It's been a pleasure knowing you, Major.'

'Likewise, Major. I wish this had a happier ending, but look at it this way—we got to see the sky again, we killed that bastard Zhang, and we died fighting, on our feet. Sometimes that's all you can hope for.'

He nodded. He knew how this worked. As a Para, you trained as hard as you could, you tried as hard as you could, and you built up your skills to a level where you entered every fight confident you would prevail. Except you knew that someday you wouldn't.

Looked like that day had finally come.

The Chinese were now making their way to us, moving from cover to cover, from tree to boulder, showing good tactical thinking. Two of them would fire a shot, keeping us cooped up, while two others would move forward. Good tactics and completely unnecessary, given the state we were in. One man, perhaps getting complacent, moved a few steps ahead of his buddy and tried to reach a rock further than the one his buddy was behind. I leaned out from behind cover and fired at him. Two shots. One or both must have got him because he went down and didn't get up. His buddies unloaded on us and we hunkered down again. Then they started their advance again.

This time we had another trick up our sleeve. Naladala leaned out from the other side, pointing his rifle at the two advancing men. They saw it and dove to the right, taking cover, not knowing he had no bullets. That broke the rhythm of their advance and brought them into my line of fire. Here I got lucky and didn't run out of ammo.

Four shots. Two fired at one man, and when I saw him go down, the other two at his companion. The first man was dead, and I'd nicked the second. He went down but managed to crawl to cover as his buddies fired again, forcing me and Naladala behind the boulder.

Naladala was grinning.

'Don't be so happy, Major.'

'Why not?'

'I'm out.'

Zero bullets against four remaining enemies. Not good odds at all.

'What now?'

Naladala and I shared a look that answered his question without me needing to say anything. Once you were a Para, you were one for life. It did something to you—instilled in you a belief that you should never give up. If you're out of bullets, use your hands; if they get your hands, use your feet; if they get your feet, use your teeth. Whatever it took till the bastards finally managed to kill you, and even then, leave them in awe of just how a Para died.

I leaned out and took a look. One of the men ran straight towards us, and dove for cover. Then another. When they didn't get a single bullet coming towards them, they broke cover and began walking straight towards us. They must have figured out we were out of ammo. In their shoes, I would have fancied my odds as well. Naladala was now holding his rifle like a club, but he was weakened and against fit, young men with guns, he would not last long. Pity that a man like him should get out of his prison only to die like this.

I leaned out again and took another look. They were no more than ten metres away and sauntering in, with the smug expression that came from knowing they had won this thing.

That was till one of their heads exploded.

They froze. A dumb thing to do, because then another guy's head exploded. The remaining two soldiers started firing at us, perhaps thinking we had something to do with their exploding heads. We took cover as bullets pinged off the boulder and all around us.

'What the fuck just happened?'

Then the bullets stopped. I took another look.

There was just one guy standing and when his last remaining buddy's head had exploded, he had realized we were not the ones doing the damage. He looked around frantically, trying to see which direction his attackers were firing from. By now his training had taken over and he knew what I did. His friends' heads had not exploded spontaneously, but because someone had taken them out with a suppressed sniper rifle. Someone very good with it.

I knew just such a man, but he was dead. Dead on a Hanoi rooftop. Or so I had believed. Then the fourth man fell, his head suffering the same fate as his friends.

The bushes ahead of us parted and a man walked into view. Wearing black fatigues, a black bandana around his head. Face smeared with black paint, cradling a Dragunov sniper rifle in his hands.

Aman Karzai.

'Major, you look like shit.' I covered the remaining few steps to Karzai and embraced him, relieved to be alive and relieved to see him alive as well. As we pulled aside, he looked a bit awkward at this display of affection. I mean, I'm not the most touchy-feely of people, but then Karzai was no longer a stranger, he was a brother, more than a brother for our bond had been tested and proven when our lives depended on us being there for each other.

'Sure beats being dead. Speaking of the dead, how the hell did you get out of that mess in the market alive?'

'We'll get to that, Major. All in good time. For now, we still need to ensure we stay alive and get out of here.'

He looked over at Naladala, who looked flabbergasted at this sudden turn of events.

'This the guy this was all about? He better be worth it.'

Naladala just kept staring at Karzai, unsure of what to say or do. Karzai made it easier by pointing at Zhang's body and then at the building we had just exited.

'I was hoping to get this bastard myself, but you got him. The next best thing. Now, any idea how many soldiers or prisoners may be left inside?'

To be honest, we had been so focused on getting out that I had no idea. I told Karzai as much.

'We'll just have to find out the hard way. Your Indian friends insisted we get any intel and files we can from in there. They weren't specific about what to do with any other prisoners, but I'm not as heartless as those spooks. If there are any, let's let them out and hope they make it out in time.'

'In time for what?'

Those were Naladala's first words since Karzai had showed up.

Karzai grinned in reply. 'Before the Indians fire a few more missiles and destroy the camp.'

Naladala's jaw dropped, and I imagined I looked no different. Having Karzai come back from the dead to our rescue when we'd thought ourselves dead was a big enough shock, and now to discover that the explosions that had aided our escape were due to Indian missiles was even more of a shock.

Karzai was a man in a hurry, apparently aware of deadlines we were oblivious of, and he began to walk towards the building, his rifle at the ready. 'Major, your arm looks really bad, but grab a pistol.'

He looked at Naladala. 'I assume you're good with a rifle.'

Naladala just nodded.

'Let's clean this place up, gentlemen, and then get the hell out of here.'

With those words, we went back into the building that we had tried so hard to get out of.

Our first port of call was Zhang's office and as we navigated the rubble left over from the earlier strikes, we saw no sign of any Chinese. Perhaps they had all gone outside when the explosions began. As Karzai put disks and files into the backpack that had been on his back, I pulled Naladala aside.

'Were there any other prisoners? I was in a cell with four pretty poor-looking sods whom they killed later.'

I could see the distaste writ large on his face.

'They would pick up tanker crews they could ransom for money, and once in a while when fishermen stumbled onto them, they would dispose them. I really don't know whether they have others, but to be honest, I never saw more than a couple of rooms they used as cells.'

'Wait here and cover Karzai in case you get company. Let me take a look around.'

My left arm was numb by now, and that was both good news and bad news. Good news because at least it was not hurting any more, bad news because numbness meant it would require some serious medical attention. The thought that I might lose my arm flashed through my mind, and I tried to dismiss it as I walked through the corridors.

The core of the building was largely intact, and I wondered how on earth they had aimed their missiles with such precision that they had not taken me out as collateral damage. Then I remembered the tracker Karzai had given me, something supposedly developed by a German company. A tracker which you ingested, and which allowed you to be tracked for 48 hours before it dissolved in your bloodstream.

Ten minutes of looking around convinced me there were no more prisoners and I was about to head back to Karzai and Naladala when I saw some movement in a corner.

Buried under the rubble, bleeding from a gash on her forehead, was Chen Yao.

Thankfully she was thin and small, otherwise there was no way I could have half-dragged, half-pulled her back to Karzai.

When he saw me, his eyes narrowed, 'That does not look like a hostage.'

'As far as I can tell, Zhang's boss. A spy or someone important in the government. I thought she had got away in the helicopter I heard taking off, but clearly she didn't get that far.'

'Major, I think I've got all that your Indian friends told me to look for, or at least as much of it as I can carry. Let's head out. If we have their boss with us, any remaining stragglers out there will be out to get us.'

I continued to drag Chen along. She was only partially conscious, but I was sure that she was worth more to Gopal than all the files we could carry back. It was slow, and painful, but if we were to get into a firefight, the two among us who could use rifles were Naladala and Karzai and it made sense for them to keep their hands free. The first hundred metres out of the compound were uneventful, and then we saw movement in the trees ahead.

'Take cover. Karzai, flank right behind that rock. Srini, left.'

We moved into combat mode. There was no second-guessing and no discussion. Karzai was a trained fighter who had seen more action that I had, but I had more experience in commanding men in battle, and with the comfort and familiarity that comes with two people who have seen battle together, without much ado, we got down to action. Naladala was rusty, weakened, but once you wear the maroon beret you never really lose the edge, so he understood and got to action, moving left and scampering behind a rock.

Six men in black uniform came rushing out, rifles in front. They must have been at the outer perimeter, and after hearing the mayhem back at their base and not getting any responses to their radio calls, they would have realized how bad things were.

I waited till they were fifty metres away, and then I walked out from behind cover, holding Chen in front of me. By now she had recovered to a large extent and began barking orders at the soldiers in Chinese. Maybe she was asking them to shoot through her, or maybe she was asking not to be shot. I had no idea what she said. Either way, the Chinese did what most soldiers in most parts of the world do when faced with the prospect of pissing off someone much higher in the totem pole. They were paralysed with indecision.

Of course, we were under no such constraints. We reported to no one, had no paperwork to fill out, and could wreak all the havoc we wanted. The first Chinese man to die was the one who had raised his rifle, perhaps the one who had the most initiative. He paid for it as Karzai took his head off. The others turned to look at their dead comrade. Then another fell as Karzai's suppressed rifle took another man in the neck.

After that mayhem as Naladala screamed something in a language I couldn't recognize but which he would later tell me were the choicest abuses in his native Kannada. The remaining four Chinese turned to face this unexpected threat to their left.

Naladala backed up his bark with some real bite as he unloaded on the four men with the AK-47 he was holding, firing on full auto.

You can do the math. An AK magazine holds thirty rounds. On full auto, it fires at six hundred rounds per minute. Blowing your mag in three seconds may be cathartic but of limited utility in a real firefight where the enemy is firing back, which is why we rarely used our rifles on full auto, using single shots or three-round bursts. However, against four tightly packed men taken completely by surprise, Naladala wreaked havoc, scything through the four. We didn't wait to check if any of them were alive, but ran past them, Karzai now joining me, grabbing Chen by an arm and hustling her along.

As we ran, I shouted out to Karzai. 'How the hell do we get out?'

'Your Indian friends have that covered.'

We continued for at least half an hour through the foliage, and reached the water without any further challenge. Karzai took out a radio from his backpack and called, saying just four words.

'Cardinal and Invictus safe.'

Invictus was of course Naladala, and Cardinal was my call sign from back in the day. Karzai was clearly calling the Indians. I turned to ask him whom, when Naladala shouted out. 'There! In the water!'

In the distance, the surface of the water was disturbed as two sleek objects came out from beneath the sea, rising vertically to a few hundred feet before their motors ignited and they turned towards us, streaking towards the island, trailing smoke. I had seen a lot of things in my time in uniform, but nothing like this. The missiles moved so fast I barely had time to register their progress before they slammed into the compound we had left. A second later, two more homed in on their target. The explosions were so powerful that we were thrown off our feet.

As we looked back, we saw a huge pillar of smoke rising into the sky. Chen was glaring at me, knowing she had lost her men and base and from being the captor was now our prisoner.

Karzai told Naladala to help cover Chen as he handed me his backpack. He was looking at me, his wry grin back. As I heard the motor of an approaching boat, I knew it was time to say goodbye.

He pointed back to the approaching speedboat with his head. 'Major, that's my ride. I can't go back. The Americans still regard me as a fugitive and who knows when the Indians would decide to hand me over to them. I really don't care what the Indians and Chinese are up to, but am glad we met. And I am glad we got some payback.'

He shook my hand and started walking towards the boat.

'Karzai.'

He turned to look at me.

'Uroor.'

His grin disappeared at my words, replaced by something deeper, more thoughtful. We had been through a lot together, but I had never called him what I just did in his native Pashto.

Brother.

He waved to me as he got into the boat. 'Take care of yourself and your family, my brother.'

And then he was gone.

Naladala nudged me. 'I do hope you have a plan to get us out of here.'

I didn't, but thankfully I didn't have to show just how out of my control the whole situation was when the water just a few hundred metres away began churning and frothing, as if a giant creature were emerging from underneath. When the leviathan did emerge and come to rest, all our jaws dropped open, especially Chen's.

We were looking at the sleek, black hull of a submarine. A speedboat left it, coming towards us, carrying four men wearing black, armed with automatic weapons. When they reached the shore, two of them came to us, stopped and saluted me and Naladala.

'We're MARCOS, sir. We're here to fetch you.'

One of them looked at Chen, his eyes widening at what I said. 'We have a gift. Our bosses may want to talk to her. She wasn't part of the original plan, but we thought we'd do some additional shopping while here. You know how tempting that cheap, made-in-China junk is.'

It wasn't that funny, but Naladala and I were so relieved that we began laughing our guts out at that lame statement. The MARCOS were looking at us curiously. We must have made a strange sight even to the hardened marine commandos of the Indian Navy. Me, a man with his arm bloodied and broken, but busy telling bad jokes; Naladala, bloodied, emaciated, dressed in rags, and who had just started singing Kannada songs. And I dare say, his singing was definitely worse than my sense of humour. On top of all that, between the two of us, we were carrying a Chinese prisoner of war wearing a designer suit and high heels.

But then, we were going home.

And we were not just two men going home.

We were Paras going home from war.

16

A little while after I boarded the sub, I passed out. When I finally woke up, it was in a hospital. The doctor told me I had been unconscious for well over a day. A couple of surgeries later my hand still hurt like hell, but the doctors concluded that they did not need to chop it off and that, over time, I might be able to make full use of it. The surgeon, who had been wearing a naval uniform, told me that he understood I had been shot, but how had I suffered the other wound above my elbow? By then, exhausted, hurt and not giving a rat's ass about how Gopal and his spooks would spin the story, I told him a Chinese assassin had tried to stab me and I had used my own hand as a shield before I took out the knife and stabbed the Chinese guy in the neck.

The surgeon had stopped asking me questions after that.

I was sitting on the hospital bed, pestering the doctors about when I could call my family and not getting much by way of answers, when the door opened and two men stood before me. Ajay Gopal and MK Dhar.

Dhar walked up to me and ran his hand over my hair, an uncharacteristic paternal gesture. 'You did it, my boy. You did it.'

I wasn't sure what he meant. Did he mean I'd managed to rescue Naladala, or that I'd killed Zhang, or that I'd brought a bunch of intelligence back with me, or that I'd brought back Chen Yao? Looking at Gopal's eyes, I was about to say something rude, but clearly with Dhar, it was different. He sat next to me on the bed and held my hand.

'My grandson is also called Aaditya, as I told you once. If anything had happened to you, I don't think I would have forgiven myself.'

For Dhar, it was enough that I had got back in one piece. In a world where people like me were just pawns, it was good to know someone gave a damn. Gopal walked up to me, a wary look in his eyes.

'Major, you may believe a lot of things about men like me. That we send soldiers like you to die in wars we start, or that we see you as just expendable tools.'

I said nothing and, after an awkward silence, continued. 'What happened back at that base and in Hanoi?'

So I told him. He winced when I told him about how Krishnan had betrayed us. It was a bit of a shock to me that he was not at all surprised at the role Karzai had played. Gopal whispered something to the MARCOS commando at the door and a second later a man in a civilian suit came in. 'Kundu, prep the prisoner. I'll meet with her after I'm done here.'

'What will happen to her?'

I had brought Chen Yao with me, not thinking through

things in the heat of battle. However, having seen first-hand what it meant to be a prisoner in enemy hands, I asked Gopal what would happen to her.

'We are not like them, Major. We will not torture her. From what we gather, she is not military, but maybe an intelligence asset. We will learn more and take it from there.'

'Naladala?'

'He's fine. He will be debriefed and then sent back home.'

'What about me?'

Gopal smiled. 'Soon, Major. We were just waiting to make sure your health is okay. I will stay for some time with the prisoner and bring her back, but Dhar Saab is here only to get you home and back to your family.'

Dhar gently touched my shoulder. 'I have already spoken to Zoya and Ravi and told them you are safe. You can call them soon and we will take a flight home together. Just get dressed—there is a fresh set of clothes there—and join me outside.'

There were a bunch of questions in my mind. Where was I? Dhar had mentioned a flight. Was I in some military hospital in some other city?

As I walked out of the room, I found myself in a narrow corridor and we walked through it and up some stairs to a door.

Gopal held my right elbow. 'Major, you're still a bit weak and, if you don't mind, I can help you. It's a bit windy out there and I don't want you losing your footing.'

What was he talking about? Then the door opened,

and I stood there with my mouth open. I was on a wide deck, with the sea on both sides. The deck was lined with fighter aircraft and helicopters and in front of me stood a tall man wearing a Naval officer's uniform, ringed by other Navy officers. He saluted me and as I replied in kind, he shook my hand.

'It has been an honour to have you on board, Major. We thank you for your service.'

I blurted out. 'Where am I?'

He answered, a twinkle in his eye. 'Why, you have been enjoying the hospitality of our home away from home. I am Captain Sonny Iqbal, commanding officer of *INS Vikramaditya*.'

I got a tour of the aircraft carrier and had lunch with Iqbal and his officers, most of whom were clearly curious to know more about what I had been up to, but wary about asking too much in Gopal's presence. Soon after lunch, Iqbal told me my flight home was ready.

Gopal pulled me aside. 'Major, before you go home, I think you need to get out of those civilian clothes. I brought something a bit more appropriate.'

I looked in the box he handed me. It contained my old uniform, complete with all my medals and decorations and the maroon beret of the Indian Para Special Forces. I felt a lump rise in my throat. Those who have never put on a uniform would not understand, but I gripped the box tightly. What was inside was not just a set of clothes, but an identity. My identity.

Dhar winked at me. There was only one way Gopal could have got my old uniform—Dhar would have got it from Zoya. She knew I was safe and I was walking home. I put on the uniform, adjusted the beret on my head and walked out to meet Gopal and Dhar.

Our walk to the flight deck was a bit embarrassing. Most of the crew seemed to have lined up. On the way, I also saw the MARCOS who had fetched me from the island. They saluted as I walked past. Gopal and Dhar were flanking me.

'Sir, was this necessary?'

Gopal looked at me through the corner of his eyes. 'Word spreads, Major. We wouldn't want these sailors to know everything, but they know you brought back one of our own from behind enemy lines. They saw the state you were in and the shape Naladala was in, and they saw Chen.'

Dhar winked at me. 'Enjoy it, son. As with all young soldiers, such tales grow in the telling. I've overheard a couple of the MARCOS say you took on a whole company of Chinese.'

I saluted the men near me as Dhar and I got into the helicopter. Soon, we were airborne. Dhar took out a satellite phone from the bag he was carrying. 'Aadi, you can call Zoya soon. We didn't want you to call her from the carrier. We wouldn't want the Chinese to know you were here.'

As the giant aircraft carrier receded behind us, I turned to Dhar. 'Sir, I still can't get over it. I served in the army for over a decade, and I would never have imagined submarines launching cruise missiles and sending an aircraft carrier just to get back a couple of men. I mean…'

He interrupted me. His eyes were hard. 'You mean that

people like me would not give a shit about soldiers like you?'

I tried to say something, but to be honest that was exactly what I thought. Dhar grinned. 'Relax, I'm only yanking your chain. I wouldn't blame you for thinking that. Our government has often left our soldiers in the lurch, but things are changing. Gopal is a ruthless man, and our prime minister is ambitious, focused and ruthless in his own way, but at least they are patriotic. Let me put it this way, with men like them, at least I can say that they deserve to have young men like you in uniform, because they won't just throw you away when their work is done.'

I thought that over, and back to how my army career had ended, when I and my unit had been accused of war crimes, been crucified by the media, and our own government had done nothing to back us up. What the government seemed to have done for me and Naladala did go some way in washing away those ugly memories.

When I looked at Dhar, his grin had widened. 'Plus, your friend Karzai drives a hard bargain. He was the one who got New Delhi to commit and gave them a plan they could work on.'

'What do you mean, sir?'

'He got in touch with me directly after you were taken in Hanoi. He was wounded, but not too badly. Told me what had happened. Also told me he could track you but could not extract you by himself.'

Dhar looked out the window at the sea below. Usually his eyes were twinkling, almost like a schoolboy up to some mischief nobody had yet discovered. What I saw on his face now was a look of admiration. 'Imagine a man who is officially wanted as a terrorist reaching out to me. Imagine him then getting on a call with the Indian National Security Advisor requesting help.'

Karzai had placed himself in terrible danger. For all he knew, the Indians could have taken him. But then I knew what Dhar was perhaps now realizing. There were men like Karzai, who might not have served a flag or worn a uniform, but were driven by something much more powerful—a sense of honour. I took a deep breath as I realized just how much Karzai had done for me.

Dhar looked back at me and continued. 'As you may imagine, Gopal struck a hard bargain. He wanted any intel Karzai got, and when Karzai began talking about us helping with firepower and not just with reconnaissance through drones, he offered Gopal something he couldn't refuse—a hard disk he had with intel about Operation Camel. We've decrypted it and we have a treasure trove of Chinese operatives whom we can now roll up.'

'How will we get away with firing cruise missiles at Chinese troops?'

The twinkle in Dhar's eyes was back and he grinned. 'What troops? That was just an uninhabited island, as per the Chinese. There was no camp, and no Chinese soldiers. Our submarine suffered a malfunction and had to eject its weapons to avoid an explosion onboard. They chose an island in international waters where nobody lived.'

'The Chinese will be hopping mad, and they will not let it rest.'

'We have more leverage now with the lady you brought back. We'll see how that plays out. Now, enough talking shop. Your family is waiting to hear from you.'

He handed me a sat phone and I dialled Zoya's number. I found my hand shaking as the phone rang. 'Zo.'

'Aadi! Oh God, I missed you.'

More than everything else that had happened, hearing her voice made it all real.

I was going home.

'To Aaditya. May he never go off on his quests again!'

Ravi raised his glass in a toast, and grimaced as he lifted his arm. Zhang had cut him deep, and he would take time to fully recover. Still, the mischief in his eyes was back, and it was good to have him and Rekha over, back in our own home.

A week had passed since I had come home. My left arm was in a cast, but the doctors had said they anticipated a full recovery. We had moved back home just two days ago, under the watchful eyes of half a dozen cops. Those cops were still outside the society gate and the walls. Sitting inside our home, surrounded by the people I loved, it was easy to believe that things were back to normal. However, I wondered if they ever would be.

'Or if he insists on going on quests, he gets back in one piece.' That toast was raised by Phadke, who had just emerged from the kitchen after pouring himself a glass of single malt.

I raised my wine glass to him. 'I'm done with quests.'

Zoya had been bringing out a fresh batch of pakodas, and stepped past Phadke and sat next to me on the sofa, where I was with Aman, who was playing with a toy car, which ever so occasionally would launch a kamikaze attack aimed at my glass.

Zoya put her arms around me and nuzzled her head against my shoulder. 'No more quests, okay?'

I kissed her forehead. 'No more quests.'

'That's what you always say.'

I was about to say something in protest when she smiled at me. 'But I'm glad you went on this quest.'

Ravi, now a few too many glasses down, raised another toast. 'To a true soldier's wife!'

After I'd come back to Mumbai and spent a couple more days with specialists at the hospital, Dhar had called Zoya, Ravi and Phadke into a meeting, telling them what had happened. Of course, he scrubbed some details and made it sound like I had been part of a rescue mission, and thankfully left out the portions about how I had been taken captive, tortured and almost died. Also, he said nothing of a certain Chinese lady I had brought back as part of my carry-on luggage.

I had many things against spooks, but once I'd heard of this meeting, I had them to thank for something. First, they had clearly saved my life, and now taken a risk in disclosing information they would otherwise not have, and that meant I would not have to lie to those whom I cared about the most.

The TV was on and Varsha Singh was on, talking about the recently announced Chinese withdrawal from border areas.

'Experts are saying this is a triumph for Indian diplomacy. Despite the occasional grave provocation from across the border, the Indian government reacted in a mature way, preferring to resolve issues across the table. As a result, the Chinese have agreed to dismantle their forward posts which had been the immediate cause of the friction.'

I couldn't help but grin. Clearly the Indian government had got a lot of intel from the material we had recovered and the leverage that gave them over the Chinese, had convinced Beijing to play nice on border issues. I wondered where Chen Yao was. Had the Indian government even told them they had her? Had she been a bargaining chip in all the negotiations that led up the Chinese withdrawal? I smiled as I thought of all the games spooks played.

Phadke caught my expression and came and sat next to me. He leaned towards me and whispered. 'Major, be careful. It's one thing to be caught up in things. Quite another to start enjoying the chaos.'

Now a glass or two over my usual limit, I raised a quiet toast to him. 'To chaos, Ashutosh. To chaos. If it helps right some of what's wrong around us.'

He shook his head sadly. 'You have gone over to the dark side, my friend. You really think they will not call upon you again? You realize why I was briefed? They've given you Z-level security. You're officially one of theirs again.'

I sat back, thinking of the years I had spent in an office cubicle, trying to pretend to be something I was not. Then of being on the run with Karzai, trying to keep those I loved alive. I remembered the policeman who had taken a bullet for me when I had been betrayed by Sai; and I remembered Naladala.

Phadke was wrong on one count. It wasn't the chaos I enjoyed. The chaos I dealt with because it was one of the few things I was good at. What I enjoyed was being back among men who lived and died for things larger than quarterly results or project deadlines. Not for abstract concepts of patriotism, but for their brothers-in-arms.

It was the closest thing I had to a normal day nowadays. Another month had gone by. Zoya had returned to work, Aman was back at his preschool, and I was officially unemployed. After Randhawa's and Godbole's deaths and the chaos at work, my employers had decided that with their CEO and CFO killed, they needed to reassess how risky their business was. Their board of directors had decided that while being a state-run enterprise meant working closely with the government, having your executives killed made you a markedly less attractive place to work. That also meant that a man of my dubious talents was quietly handed a pink slip.

I had been fired numerous times in my life, but for the first time, I'd been just plain fired.

To be honest, I didn't give a shit. Sitting in an office, pretending to do important work is highly overrated. Gopal and his bosses had been very generous, and a large sum of money had been deposited in my account. That helped, as did the fact that Zoya was doing really well. That gave me time to spend with Aman and pursue more seriously the neighbourhood self-defence training I gave kids. The security men we had near our home and accompanying Aman to school helped, but I thought what helped Zoya really get back into her stride was knowing that I would be there for her and Aman.

As I cooked dinner—and yes, that was another skill I was picking up, my repertoire having expanded dramatically beyond Maggi—I turned on the TV and went into the kitchen to make myself some coffee.

I came back into the living room and froze as I saw a familiar face on the screen. Chen Yao.

I turned the volume up, but the news anchors had moved on to another story. I grabbed my laptop and started searching for her name, and got no hits.

When I looked up the news sites, I saw a news item on CNN. Cindy Yao, a Chinese national, was found dead in New York City the previous night. Officials were tight-lipped about her identity, but conspiracy sites on the internet were buzzing with speculation that she was a high-level Chinese operative who had somehow come into US custody or made a deal with the authorities for asylum. Unverified reports said that she was the daughter of a high-ranking Communist Party official in China. The US authorities dismissed such speculation and the Chinese government had made no comment.

My mind was reeling at what I read, and then I realized I had been thinking too literally. Spooks like Gopal wouldn't just negotiate with the Chinese for Chen. A high-ranking spy like her would be a gold mine of intelligence to the Americans. Maybe after getting what they wanted, India had traded her. God knew what concessions they'd got from the Americans. Either way, the Americans must have made their own deal with her in turn for the intel she had to offer. While the Indians and Americans played their game of 'pass the spy', the Chinese couldn't really say much, could they? A spy who did not exist, leading an operation that did not exist, had been caught in an Indian operation to free a prisoner who did not exist from a camp that did not exist. I laughed aloud at the absurdity of the whole situation.

That laughter disappeared when I clicked to read the rest of the story. Her death caused a sensation, as it occurred in broad daylight as she was walking in Central Park. Bystanders noted that there were two men in dark suits walking near her. Conspiracy theorists were quick to identify these men as US agents, but with little supporting evidence.

I smiled as I got back to cooking after reading once again the last line of the news article.

Ms Yao was killed by a single shot to the head, fired by an unknown sniper.

EPILOGUE

'Mom, can I have a cake pop, please?'

Rachel Harmening smiled. She would have bought the boy sitting at the table behind her anything he had asked for at that moment. For he had finally called her 'mom' in public.

The barista across the counter looked at her and grinned. 'Beautiful day, isn't it?'

'You bet. Get me a Caramel Frappuccino, an orange juice and a couple of those cake pops.'

As she walked back to the table, the boy looked up at her and smiled. 'Two?'

'Yup.'

As he devoured his snacks, Rachel just looked at him. She had brought Hanif back to the United States almost two years earlier, after the events in Afghanistan when she had been taken hostage and then rescued. Hanif had been Aman Karzai's protégé, and he had asked her to give him a better life than he could have had in Afghanistan. The formalities for adopting him had been recently completed, and while it had taken Hanif a while to get used to it, now calling her 'mom' was natural for him. He was thirteen and looked nothing like the scrawny kid she had brought back. Better nutrition had meant he had filled out and was rapidly growing in height. With his baseball cap, sweatshirt and jeans, he looked like any other teenager at the Starbucks, out with his mom.

'Kiddo, when will you get back?'

Hanif looked up at her and swallowed the piece of cake pop in his mouth. 'I'll be done with Jacob's birthday party in a couple of hours. Don't worry, I remember I need to prepare for that math test. I've got it under control. And yeah, I'll call you when I reach Jacob's. It's like only a block away, so don't stress.'

'I won't. I'll hang around here working on my article. Just get back here when you're done and we can check out the Museum of Natural History like you wanted, grab a bite and then get back home.'

'Got it, Mom!'

With that, he kissed her on the cheek and ran out of the Starbucks. Rachel was looking at the still-swinging door, her eyes misting over, when she sensed someone slide into the chair in front of her.

'He was always a good kid, and you're doing an amazing job of raising him.'

Rachel swung around and gasped as she saw the man in front of her. When she had last seen him, he had been wearing dust-covered clothes. Now, in his neatly pressed blue shirt and trousers, he looked like an office-goer who had stepped out for a Saturday afternoon coffee from his Manhattan office. His greying hair had been matted and dirty, now it was close-cropped and gelled into place. However, his piercing blue eyes were the same, as was the wry grin on his face.

'Oh, my God, Aman. What are you…?'

He reached across the table and she caught her breath, thinking he was going to hold her hand. Instead, he passed on a pen-drive to her. And then, to her surprise, he did close his hand over hers. 'Rachel, thank you for everything you've done for him, and for me. This drive has info I got that you may find useful. Links to some American corporates who may be better taken down by your methods.'

Rachel had been in touch with Aman on the internet and through coded messages, but this was the first time she had seen him in person since Korengal. A million contradictory thoughts crossed her mind. The man in front of her was, according to the US government, a wanted killer. However, he was also a man of honour. He was the rare man who was driven not by what he gained, but by doing what was right. She had never asked him what he did with the information he gathered, but the growing list of sniper killings she had tracked over the years made it amply clear what he had been up to.

She didn't necessarily agree with all his methods, but admired him for his sense of duty and selflessness and, over time, that admiration had grown into something more.

'It was great seeing Hanif and seeing you.'

'Stay. Meet Hanif. He still talks about you.'

Karzai shook his head. 'The life I gave him is not what

he deserves. He deserves a better one—the one you can give him. It's perhaps better that he forgets me over time.'

As he made to retract his hand, Rachel held on. 'You've done more than any one man can be expected to. Why don't you stop? When will you stop? Why don't you stay with us? We could…'

She fumbled. How could they ever have a normal life? The US government would come after Karzai for his past deeds, and the enemies he had made would never truly let them be safe.

Karzai must have read her mind and he laughed. 'You need to understand, Rachel. I have done terrible things. I have killed innocent people and the only way I can atone for those sins is to bring those behind that evil to justice. When that's done…'

Rachel held onto his hand. 'When you feel that's done, I don't want you to think you have nothing to live for. Come to us.'

He nodded and then put on dark sunglasses and a cap and stood, putting on a bulky overcoat. 'I'll be in touch. Take care.'

On impulse, she got up and hugged him. He flinched. He was not used to anyone showing emotions for him, and it had been a long time since he had allowed himself to show emotions towards anyone.

As she stepped back, he smiled at her. 'Don't worry about me. I'll be okay. I'm thinking of spending some time in this part of the world, and before I leave, I promise to look you up.'

'That would be nice. Take care.'

He walked toward the counter where a barista stood, looking with a puzzled expression at the takeaway cup he held in his hand, trying to make sense of the name written on the side. 'Excuse me, I think that is mine.'

The young barista looked at the man in front of him. Looked like a banker with the fancy coat and formal shirt and trousers. 'Man, this your lucky number or something?'

The man wearing the sunglasses smiled as he leaned on the counter. 'Something like that.'

The barista shrugged. Rich bankers had a weird sense of humour, he surmised. 'Okay, lemme get you your drink. It's ready.'

He poured the coffee into the cup and handed it to the man.

'Here you are, man. Brewed coffee to go for Mister Seven Six Two.'

Mainak Dhar

Mainak Dhar wears many hats. He considers his most important job to be the best possible father and husband he can be. An alumnus of the Indian Institute of Management, Ahmedabad, he has worked in the corporate world for over two decades, and his 'day job' has been leading businesses in the corporate world. A self-described 'cubicle dweller by day and writer by night', when he's not with his family or at work, he loves creating and sharing stories. He is the author of over a dozen books, some of which have been bestsellers in India and abroad including the bestselling *Alice in Deadland* series, 03:02 and *Sniper's Eye*. His books have been translated into Turkish, Vietnamese, Japanese, French, German and Portuguese, reaching millions of readers worldwide. He is also a passionate student of Karate and holds a Black Belt. Learn more about him at **www.mainakdhar.com.**